Leaks, Lies, Lust and Love

CHERYL BARTON

Leaks, Lies, Lust and Love

Leaks in order to right a criminal wrong.

Lies to cheat and then steal from the fortunate and the unfortunate.

Lust so insatiable that amorous fantasies lead to sensual seduction.

Love so unforgettable that the scars of the past can't outweigh reignited desires of the here and now.

Dear Reader,

Here we are, seven books in with the *Brothers of Chi-Town* romance series. I'm still just as excited as I was when I started the series with Carter and Sienna Garrison's rekindled love story in *I Can't Let Go*. We then ventured in to the sexiest of the relationships, with Torrence Allen and Reese Michaels in *Swagger and Baggage*. I cannot forget about Dexter Patterson and Alyssa Kincaid's love story and how he fought for the love of his life and the child he didn't know he needed until he did in *Claiming His Child*. We took a trek in *Always Bet on Black* with Delvin 'DJ' Michaels and Avalon Hart where crime actually did pay for them. Next up was the plunge into love via a rocky road in *It Takes Two to Tangle* with Tucker Glass and Nichelle Michaels. Let's not forget the world's sexiest wrestler, down for the count after a clash or what was an actual crash between Joey Kincaid and Marlow Warren in *Crashing Into Love*. We're now at the next in the series, *Leaks, Lies, Lust and Love* with Carlos Kincaid and Everly Robinson discovering that love a second time around can be the sexiest of all.

I'm glad you're still rocking with me because the series isn't over yet. There is one more, *Love's Gamble* with Horace Grant and Angel Reagan's story. You can preorder your copy now, ahead of the release.

We're also going to check back in with everyone from the previous books to see how their lives have turned out in that amazing city called ***Chicago***!

If you're new here, you can get the first six books right now at https://www.cherylbarton.net/the-brothers-of-chi-town-series

Thanks for coming along and staying on this journey with me!

Cheryl

Dedication

Wow, this has been some year. I questioned whether I would get back to writing before the end of the year. Here I am, reaching back and feeling the love of family who have left my presence but never my heart.

I dedicate all the love I have poured into this story to my father, John A. Barton, Jr, my brother, John A. Barton, III and to my cousin, Andrea Denise Gentry. I miss you all greatly. I continue to thrive because you once lived.

Rest sweetly. I will never forget.

1

Carlos Kincaid used his finger to scan over the notes in his iPad. Sitting around the conference room of the *Fight or Flight Private Security Agency* that he co-owned with his brother, Joey Kincaid, were the top six guys who made up the leadership in the company. Though the company had been up and running for a while, they were finally expanding to accommodate the increasing number of new clients who sought out their services. For years, his focus has been on the company while Joey stayed around as more of a consultant. With his career taking off as a professional wrestler in a world where he was known as, *Joey Dreads*, because of the long dreadlocks he wore as his signature look, he focused more on his life-long passion of going pro. Still, he kept a foot in the company and weighed in heavily on the direction they were going in.

With the recent acquisition of a contract to assist in the security of the newly elected mayor of Chicago, Tucker Glass and his wife, Nichelle, they had also been tapped for new work, some as a result of referrals by Tucker.

Adding to their current heavy work load, they had just obtained the contract to provide security for Torrence Allen's second casino where the construction was about to begin. It was important that the site be protected around the clock, especially from trespassers who wanted to get a closer look.

The agency had already accepted the job as head of security at Torrence's first Chicago casino, the *Montiel Avage Hotel and Casino*, Chicago West location. The new casino, under the same name, would be the Chicago East location. With Torrence temporarily out of full-time commission, but handling some work when he can due to his wife, Reese going through a complicated pregnancy, his best friend, Horace Grant had just moved to Chicago to temporarily oversee the new construction. Horace was part owner and general manager of their first casino located in Las Vegas. There was a lot going on and a lot the security agency was responsible for. That didn't account for the additional personal work they did that wasn't connected directly to their group of friends. Some of the guys who worked for him were hired to work at the casino. Others were spread out amongst other contracts.

Carlos enjoyed having women and men on his team of the highest caliber and skill because he trusted them with his life. With that, he trusted them with everything.

Thankful to his own sister, Alyssa Kincaid-Patterson, he was able to meet and connect with Torrence and the rest of their crew of powerful men in Chicago which soared the company's profit margin through the roof. One of those in the crew was Alyssa's husband, Dexter Patterson who he now considered as close as a brother. Their initial meet and greet wasn't the most cordial after he and Joey jumped Dex when they thought he'd gotten their sister pregnant and left her to fend for herself. That turned out to be a happy ending and a new beginning for them all.

Their love had netted him two nephews whom he loved more than life itself. He looked forward to teaching them some wrestling moves to the chagrin of their sister.

Realizing his mind was wandering, he looked around the room at several pairs of eyes that were glued on him, probably trying to figure out why he stopped talking while looking like he was miles away with his thoughts.

"Sorry about that. My mind went to a totally distant frontier. Where was I?" he asked in general.

"You were about to tell us about the long list of interviews you and Joey have coming up. You said something about a lot of positions that are left to fill with the new contracts you have in place."

Carlos nodded to Melvin Simpson, one of his lead security officers. Melvin had been with him from the first day of launching his agency. He'd been honorably discharged from the army and was in search of a place to continue to hone on his skills while keeping him closer to home+. Melvin thought of re-enlisting but felt that ten years had been enough time to dedicate fully to his country. He now wanted to give his wife and their four kids more of his time and attention. With the love of his life, Chrissy, taking care of two sets of twins every day, he wanted to be closer to them. His attention to details that not many other people noticed made him a major asset to the team.

"Thanks, Melvin."

"No problem. I think it's an old age thing," he joked.

"Funny," Carlos jibed.

He smiled when everyone around the table laughed out loud at the dig Melvin often took with him. Thankfully he took it all in stride. Melvin had come to be one of his best friends.

"Did Valerie pass the security clearance?" Deidra asked. She was one of the toughest security officers who worked for him. She was known for reminding everyone that her best friend was the Glock 22 she never left home without. Though she was known to have at least three weapons on her at any given time, that was her favorite.

"She did. In fact, sixteen of the applicants have passed. We still have a list of potentials that we're waiting on their final clearance. Until then, those who have passed still need to finish the interview process with me and with Joey."

"Is he planning to come through today? I have some information on a woman he asked me to look into," Andre, another officer asked.

"Is that about Marlow's sister, Angel?"

"Yes."

"Any luck?"

Carlos tried to stay connected to that situation that was important to him. Marlow was his brother's fiancé. Her sister was missing. Marlow had received a call from Angel after having no contact for well over a year. The call only lasted a few seconds but it was enough for Marlow to want help locating her. He would do anything for her and his brother. Getting someone on the case was a priority.

"Not much, but I have traced the phone. I may have a small lead," Andre noted.

"That's good to hear," Carlos said happily.

While he meant what he said, it was good news, it also reminded him of the night of the call from Angel to Marlow which wasn't the only eventful thing that happened that very night. He quickly turned his thoughts to Everly Robinson, the woman he once loved who had suddenly ended their relationship and left him for his best friend, Harrison Briggs. Out of nowhere, after no contact, she showed up in Chicago asking for his help with something that had to do with Hamiton. They were two people he never wanted to hear of again. His anger hadn't waned. The buck stopped at helping her with anything; until it didn't.

He was staying busy to try and forget about her. It was hard to do, but he had to do something to stay away from being in her presence now that she was staying at the very hotel that was a part of the casino where he spent most of his time as head of casino and hotel security. After a week, he was doing a pretty good job of avoiding her. He was surprised at how easy it was to move about the hotel and casino without running into her. He didn't just work, but he also lived in a two-bedroom suite at the casino. Doing so helped him stay close to work in case he was needed by his team.

"I'll run everything by Joey," Andre added.

"He should be here shortly. Marlow had another doctor's appointment, which is where he is," Carlos responded.

"I need to talk to him too about the change in his security for his next wrestling match," OC, another member of the team said.

"I spoke to him last night. He mentioned she still wasn't feeling well after collapsing a week ago after that call from her sister. She said the shock of hearing Angel's voice was overwhelming. She'd been desperate for so long to know that Angel was still alive somewhere. Hopefully, she's doing okay," Carlos said.

"Andre, if you need some help with Marlow's case on her sister, let me know. I've got some bandwidth," Deidre offered.

"Sounds good," Andre acknowledged.

"Now, back to the work at hand. After the interviews are done and the new hires are on board, I want to pair each one of them with one of you for at least three months. I want them to know how we do things. They will already have the keen skills I want our team members to have. What they need to learn is the Carlos and Joey way of doing things. People are our priority, always. Eyes and ears on all details around them while keeping their third eye on the client. One such client is a Chicago Bears player. He's the new quarterback. He didn't think he would need the kind of overly-cautious protection that we offer. He's had second thoughts about that," Carlos explained.

"That was until he was almost trampled while out at a club. He thought he was still a regular person from his old neighborhood," Melvin said.

Carlos nodded his agreement. He tried to tell the young player what he should expect but he wouldn't listen. He's listening now.

"Correct. He thought he could go back and hang with his boys from the hood and not get touched. He was wrong. Because we provide security for two other players, he's asked us to come on board to help him too. This is a job for someone who is open to traveling with the team. Eric, I'm thinking about you," Carlos said, looking and pointing in the direction of one of his earliest recruits.

"You got the right one!" Eric exclaimed. "Free travel and on-the-field view of the game? You bet I'm in. You good if I bring in two guys as lookouts?"

"I'm good with that. Take who you need. Check with Joey on the details. He'll connect you with his manager. He knows more about the player than I do. They are friends," Carlos said. "We have a lot on our plates which is why we need to get new hires onboard as soon as possible. Melvin, I want you to make sure the new team members go through your alert training. That's as important as gun training. Speaking of that, Deidra, get everyone coming on board time on the gun range."

The conference room door opened. All heads turned to Joey as he entered.

"All hail the Dragon of Dreads!" Melvin shouted and saluted as if Joey were royalty.

"Yeah, yeah. What have I missed?" he asked, taking the seat at the head of the table where Carlos usually sat.

"Apparently the chair you usually sit in," Carlos joked.

"It's unoccupied!" Joey exclaimed with his feet now resting on the top of the table.

"You're the only other person I'd let sit in my seat. Yes, you've missed a lot. I'll bring you up to speed in a minute. We're actually wrapping up. Questions anybody?" Carlos asked.

After thumbs up from everyone in the room, Carlos did the same with his thumb, signaling the meeting was over. The room quickly emptied out as everyone, he was sure, was heading to their own offices, leaving him and Joey alone. He looked at his watch hoping he could get out of the office and back to the casino within the hour. He had a meeting with that team. Being in their own off-site building gave him more of a reprieve from running into Everly. He hated that he couldn't go a few hours without thinking about her. For some reason, he felt that most of the chat he and his brother were about to have was going to be about Everly. He hated the thought, but welcomed the input on what he's been going through since she returned.

2

"Interesting week, huh?" Joey asked. His own life has been a rollercoaster as much as anyone else's who was at the casino the night Carlos' past paid him an unexpected visit.

"Understatement. Life is absolutely crazy right now. I'm working on getting a handle on it."

Carlos was lying. Even when he tried to hide his vulnerabilities from others, they never escaped Joey's prying eyes. Carlos moved to a seat at the table where he'd placed his laptop when he first entered the room. He avoided eye contact by flipping through the computer screens. He heard Joey chuckling knowing his penchant for reading him through his eyes and finding everything that was on his mind.

"Right. I see you, bro. Don't try that eye thing with me. You'll lose every time. Have you talked to her today?"

"Nope," Carlos quickly shot back without looking up.

"Are you going to? It's been a week now. Everly has been back in Chicago and at the casino hotel for a week and you're telling me that you haven't had even one sighting of her? Don't you think you should have a heart-to-heart with her? I mean, I know what she did, but she's here. Your inquiring mind doesn't want to know why she's asking for your help? You don't want to know where she's been? What's she's been doing? Nothing?" Joey prodded.

"I don't think so. No reason to find out anything from her directly. I spoke with Marlow this morning when she called to check on me. I love her for you. Have I told you that?"

Joey paused. It was clear Carlos wanted to change the subject. He would give him a reprieve for a few moments. It wasn't often they had a lot of time to chat with their busy schedules. He was surprised that he had time to stop by the office today after tending to Marlow. Nothing mattered but her health and well-being. He decided to play along by letting him off the hook.

"Yes, you have told me that. She's the perfect woman. I was lost until we found each other.

"How is she feeling? She had an appointment this morning, right? A week later and she was still reeling from hitting her head when she fell? I should probably give her another call today to check on her. She will be my sister-in-law soon. That will make her family. You know how I am about family. Alyssa says I'm still overprotective of her and she's married with kids now."

Carlos laughed to himself and leaned back. Joey wagged a finger at him. He wasn't going to win the changing of the subject game.

"Stop trying to distract me with useless chatter. Marlow is fine. We will both forever be looking out for our sister. Why haven't you talked to her? I'm going to keep bringing up Everly until you talk to me."

Carlos got up and walked over to turn on the Keurig. He needed a cup of coffee before diving into the conversation that his brother wasn't going to let him escape from.

"I don't have anything to say. Marlow said the two of you got her a room but that Torrence comped it for as long as she needs to stay there."

"Yeah. I called and thanked him. I actually spoke to him while I was driving here. He didn't have to do that. He doesn't even know Everly. None of us know her like you do. Everly was your world," Joey explained.

"Until she wasn't. Have you forgotten about that?" Carlos asked.

Joey saw the vein in Carlos' neck stand out. He was getting angry as they conversation went on. He didn't want that. He did want his brother to talk out what was going through is head. It was the only way he'd be able to focus on what is important.

"I haven't forgotten. She is here. She needs help and we're giving it to her. Our sister, who I never thought would reach out to assist the woman she vowed to hate after what she did to you, extended a hand. She then reached out to Reese. Well, you know how close Alyssa and Reese are. They went with Marlow to get Everly settled into a room. She didn't have any place else to go. She has no one else."

"Alyssa? She didn't throw a few punches at Everly? Was there a fight? A few choice curse words?" Carlos jokingly asked.

There was no doubt that at one point, Alyssa hated to hear Everly's name.

"Funny. I wasn't sure what Alyssa's reaction would be knowing Everly was in Chicago again. When you and Everly split and Alyssa heard about the circumstances, she flipped out. There weren't too many derogatory names that she hadn't come up with to call her. She was, as usual, the over-protective sister. Everly was not one of her favorite people. Yet, despite all of that, she was one of the first to step up to help her. I understand that night, the women were there for her and had some kind of secret girl-talk going on. Whatever was said, anything negative was put to the side because there was a woman in trouble and in need. Our nephews have softened our sister significantly," Joey kidded.

"Bet. I've noticed that too."

Carlos took his newly brewed cup of coffee and settled back into his seat.

"Do you want to know the latest? Any day now, the feds are going to come for her. They know she's no longer in New York. I don't think they know where in Chicago she is at the moment. Casino security is clear that everyone is closed-mouth on what they have seen or know."

"I doubt if they find her here. I understand they've been checking her old stomping grounds in the city for the past few days. I have a connection at the local FBI office and he gave me a heads up since he knows of my history with her. Her best friend, Cecily Adams reached out to me also. I didn't say anything because I wasn't sure who may have been listening. She said she'd received a mysterious voicemail from Everly and wondered what I knew."

Carlos didn't know the details but he knew no one needed to know her location for now.

"Alyssa said that as far as Everly knew, they believed she was still in New York until yesterday. She's on their radar, so they may have tracked her here."

"They will definitely be watching to make sure she doesn't leave back out of the country."

"Do you want to hear the latest or will I get more engagement from the brick wall behind you?"

Carlos exhaled. He wanted to know. At the same time, he wanted to distance himself from it all. He was suffering from a lack of sleep. The moment he went to his own suite, all his mind could concentration on was Everly and Hamilton; them together. He was sick of revisiting the idea of the two of them sneaking around behind his back. Being a glutton for punishment, he still hoped that things would work out for her. When he saw the terror on her face when she arrived, for a brief moment, he forgot what she had done to him and his desire to protect her kicked in. Hamilton turned out to be a snake. His eyes were opened to how much after pulling the knife out of his own back the day Everly told him she was leaving him and for whom.

"I'm listening," he finally said. Ready or not, he was about to get the low-down.

"Marlow talked to Alyssa after I dropped her off at home an hour ago. Everly isn't in handcuffs yet. Shew flew into New York under an alias. Can you believe people are still doing that? They need better training at our airports. The ladies were up late that first night. I left to go home around one in the morning and Marlow stayed with Alyssa and Reese. Sienna was going to stay but Carter insisted she leave. This pregnancy for her is turning out to be a hard one. Can you believe Reese and Sienna, best friends, are pregnant at the same time? Must be something in the water," Joey kidded.

"You're going into left field, bro," Carlos warned.

"Oh, from the brother who originally didn't want to know anything. Anyway, they talked well into the morning. Marlow went back last night because Alyssa called and asked if she was free to join her. She'd picked up a bunch of things Everly would need. What is wild is neither one of them care anything about the legal ramifications of helping Everly. Before I stray again, Marlow got home about five this morning. It's a good thing she was already scheduled to be off today for her appointment. From their talk, Marlow reached out to her friend, Duncan, whose husband, Kenneth is an attorney. It's clear that Everly is in a lot of trouble. Nothing about the situation has been anywhere in the news, though you and I both know about the chatter of who was responsible for the theft at Hamilton's father's company. It's true that Hamilton is behind the theft and Everly is connected. Law enforcement has been trying to keep things on the hush until they were sure Hamilton and Everly were not in the country. The money stolen from the retiree accounts didn't go missing until recently. That's why it hasn't been reported widespread. I checked a few sources as well and that's what I found out. Getting Everly a lawyer, it seems, is the best decision at the moment. Marlow's friend's husband doesn't handle the level of case that Everly will have to fight but he knows a good lawyer who can help. Reese also knows a good lawyer at a firm she's done some marketing for. Bottom line, she'll be represented well."

"Lawyers of the magnitude that she'll need cost some serious money. How is she going to pay for a top-tier lawyer?" Carlos said, clearly now worried.

Joey saw and felt his brother's concern and was glad to see it. He hated how cold Carlos was being about all of this. It wasn't like him to be this way, but he got it. His heart had been broken. Still, he had more to share.

"Did you know Everly's father? I understand he's in the midst of all of this. Were you aware of anything about him?" Joey questioned.

"Nothing at all. She never wanted to talk about him. I gathered there was bad blood. I only knew about her brother Dante. He has stayed in trouble so they weren't close, though she loves him very much. He was the only family she ever spoke of. As for her mother, she walked about from them when Everly was a little girl. She and her brother were sent to two different foster homes. A father? Never a word about him."

"Marlow said that Everly didn't go into a lot of detail about her troubles when it came to his involvement. Everly will be arrested. She knew it when she returned. She thought it would have been at the airport in New York. She went there looking for a friend. She then pretty much hiked her way to Chicago. Once Everly is arrested, and that will happen, an attorney will be assigned to her by the court. We can't keep her at the hotel. She's ready to turn herself in to keep all of us from getting into trouble. Marlow told her to hold out a little longer. By then, hopefully Marlow's friend will come through with a contact. I think for now, she'll only need to come up with the cost of the retainer. I don't know about the rest."

"I'll cover it."

Carlos heard the words before he realized what he was saying. It was clear from the look on Joey's face that he questioned what his own ears just heard.

"What?"

"You heard me."

"Carlos, you are a ball of confusion. You don't want to know anything and you won't talk to her, but you're willing to shell out big bucks to help her get a lawyer? How do you know that she's not guilty of what she's being accused of?"

"Did she say she didn't do it?" Carlos questioned. He knew a lot about Everly with the biggest being she would not be a part of a scheme to rob people of their life's savings; at least not willingly. Hamilton on the other hand, this was him all over the place."

"She said she was unaware of the scale in the beginning. Most of what she knows she didn't find out until it was too late. She fled back to the states under a false passport. That will also add to her troubles, but it's the least of them."

"Joey, I hear you. She has to have a lawyer. Everly said she was broke and had nothing. I'm not a cold-hearted bastard, though I should have been one after what she did to me," Carlos acknowledged. "I've moved on. She's a person we know who needs help."

"I hear you. I'm just surprised."

"Don't tell her it's me. If Marlow can get her friend to connect Everly with a good lawyer, maybe this lawyer can tell her that someone has paid the retainer who prefers to remain anonymous."

"She'll wonder if it's you."

"And you won't tell her that it is, will you?"

"Of course not. I would never betray your trust. You sure?"

"Tell Marlow to keep you posted. When you know what's needed, you're on my accounts so, take out whatever is needed. Keep this between us? Clear?" Carlos asked.

Joey nodded.

Carlos didn't know what he was doing helping the woman who was his biggest betrayer. He also wondered where Hamilton was and why he wasn't helping Everly out of this mess considering they left as a couple. He had no doubt Hamilton had roped her into something that she now had to answer for. He was ghost just as he knew he would be.

"Crystal clear."

"Good. No more about Everly right now. We have a lot to talk about when it comes to business. For starters, are you going to help me with these interviews? I've received a request from the quarterback you brought to my attention. That's being taken care of. I need to prepare for the security team who will eventually work at the new casino. That's a massive undertaking. Thankfully, we have a while before they will all need to be in place."

"We're talking about fifty to sixty staff members. The casino doesn't want to hire them directly?" Joey asked.

"No, they are okay with expanding the scope of our contract to include the large number of new hires we'll need. The current contracts for the security guys that work there are yearly. When this year is up, we're add those staff to our team and others, who don't make the cut, will be let go. Torrence and Horace want everything to go through us. I'll have our assistant reach out to our attorneys so that they can go over the new five-year contract which will cover all of their casinos including the one in Las Vegas. This is huge, but we can handle it."

"Carlos, do you know what this means? We will be employing over five hundred people. We are going to need a much larger administrative team."

"I'm all over that. Maria, Dawn and Justin, in our front office are working on the job recruitment notice. Thankfully, we have enough office space to accommodate growth. We are definitely in a major boost season."

"True and you're right; we've got this."

Carlos agreed with a thumbs up.

"For now, it's only about keeping the construction site secure. I know your wrestling schedule is about to be crazy. I'm hoping you can help out with hiring and some training before you hit the road. Do you think you have time?"

"I have all the time you need."

"Good. Go see Andre. He has some information on Marlow's sister. It's not a lot but he said he has an update."

Joey stood to leave. He was putting everything into helping Marlow find her sister. He had to do that if Marlow was going to have any peace.

"Are you heading over to the casino?" Joey asked.

"That's my plan."

"What if you run into Everly?"

"I don't know. I'm pretty good at avoidance."

"You can't do that forever. She's back in town. Soon, her face will be all over the media. You'll be seeing her everywhere. Talk to her. You asked everyone to help her. Don't walk away now."

"I hear you."

Joey left the room. He could only hope that Carlos was listening to him.

3

Everly sighed as once again, team no-sleep had consumed her. Except for maybe an hour, she'd been up the entire night contemplating how this was where her life was now. Over a year ago, she was in love and in the arms of the most amazing man she'd ever met. Her only problem was, having no family and no one to really say they loved her and cared for her, she didn't trust her love for Carlos enough to share her truth with him.

She rubbed her hands across the soft, plush blue comforter that covered the queen-sized bed in her hotel suite. She was dressed in the warm pajamas that Alyssa and Marlow had purchased and delivered to her. So much had happened over the past week that she was still trying to figure out what the next step was. For sure, she needed to turn herself in to the authorities. If they came for her before she went to them, her situation will eventually be worse. She needed them to know that she was not a willing participant in what happened. She certainly didn't get anything out of what Hamilton and her father, Arlo Campos had done. Without Hamilton holding her brother and Carlos' safety and their lives over her head, never would she have left the perfect love to join them in their money heist.

What mystified her most about her present state was that the only thing she wanted to do once she knew she had a chance to get out of South America was to get to Carlos. The way she'd left him had left her as a broken woman. Nothing was ever right again until she pulled up in front of the casino. She wasn't sure he would be there. While on the plane to New York to hopefully find refuge with Cecily Adams, one of her best friends, she read an article about the new casino and the contract that Carlos' company had received to provide security. She knew that he would be there. Carlos was a workaholic. Even if he had a team, she knew where she'd find him because he was always hands-on. She trembled at the thought of how hands on he'd been with her. She missed that; she missed him.

Seeing him for the first time once her rideshare had pulled up to the casino hotel had stunned her heart back to life. She was instantly reminded of just how much she not only missed him, but also of how hurt he must have been when she left him for his best friend. If only she could have told him the real truth, all that she had gone through may not have been. She could, right now, be in a bed similar to this one with Carlos loving her the way she missed.

Feeling sorry for herself, Everly got out of bed and headed into the bathroom to try her best to wash off the stink and disgust of ever allowing Hamilton Briggs to convince her that she had no other choice but to let him pull her away from her perfect life and into one that had become her destiny in hell. She stripped her clothes off and headed into the steam-filled shower. Placing her hands against the one wall that wasn't glass, she let the hot water cascade over her body. What was she going to do about her current predicament? She felt alone and scared. She knew coming back to the states meant risking her freedom, but she had to come. She couldn't live a life on the run, watching over her shoulder for the rest of it. She may be guilty of allowing herself to be threatened into doing things she would never risk doing, but deep down, that wasn't who she was. She needed to get back to the Everly who lived within the law.

So much had been at stake. It was clear to her now that she'd made the wrong choice. Her decision should have been to tell Carlos everything. She had to protect him. She had to protect her brother. Her father was ruthless. The fact that Hamilton had found out about him is why her entire life changed for the worse. Home in Chicago now, the only person she could think to run to for help was Carlos. Despite the hurt she knew she left him with, there wasn't anyone else. Putting her pride to the side, she left New York without being able to reach Cecily and headed straight for Carlos in Chicago. In keeping up with him, she knew that he's spent some time in Las Vegas with his brother where they were at the top of the wrestling charts. Now, he was back in Chicago; back in the city where they had fallen in love.

Her thoughts turned to her last day in South America. Just one week ago. Grabbing the shower gel, she thought back to how she was finally able to get out of that country where a plot had begun to unfold that would have cost her everything; especially her very life.

Everly could hear them talking. At her father's mansion where she and Hamilton and his men had been living for months, she decided to go for a night-time swim. She'd been feeling anxious for weeks. The issue was, she couldn't figure out why. The unsettling spirit within her was getting worse.

To avoid the men strolling the grounds with guns, she decided to slip out of her ground level balcony that led to a path to some steps that she would have to climb to then go down the other side. No one would see her and she would be able to swim in peace.

The moment she reached the top of the stairs, she could hear her father and Hamilton talking. The topic of the discussion was her. Thankful that she was in her bare feet and they expected her to be sleeping since it was the middle of the night, she moved her body closer to the opened balcony door of her father's office and listened.

"We're going to need fake identification and passports. The authorities are getting close. What about the money?" Hamilton asked.

"The money is safe. Trust me."

"Arlo, I don't trust you. I don't trust anyone. A man who would give me information to bribe his only daughter into helping me can't be trusted. If you would throw her under the bus, there is no telling what you would do to me. All I want to do is disappear while having enough money to live a life of luxury in a place where no one will find me. I went through a lot to get that money. With your help I was able to get it out of a United States bank while keeping it untraceable and off of anyone else's radar until recently. That just shows that electronic tracking can be manipulated in a way that paper can't. Thank goodness for technology."

"Hey, Arlo Campos doesn't trust anyone, let alone you. I'm working on the papers to get us both out of here. You know someone will eventually have to take the fall. My vote is Everly."

"Man, you are hardcore cold as freaking ice. But then, you kids didn't fall far from that tree. You have a son involved with human trafficking and a daughter who is a crooked lawyer."

"True. Without you knowing that, how else would you have been able to use her to get us here? About her. We both know she has to disappear. Luckily everything leads straight to her. If she talks, she'll tell the U.S. authorities about us. You have any problems with what the plan is for her? She's to never leave this country," Arlos said.

"Cold and quite brutal."

"I'm here for business, Hamilton. I thought you were too."

"I'm all about business. You're expected to at least care about your kids. As for me, she means nothing to me; never has."

"Yet, you played the game to make your arch rival jealous by taking away his woman. He still thinks you married her?"

"Sending him the fake papers that Everly and I got married was my icing on the cake. He thought we've been friends all of these years. I've always hated the guy. Finding out that I could strip everything from his life was payback for him always having a leg up on me since we were young. My own father even thought more of, and celebrated him more than he did me. Because of him, I missed out on what could have been a lucrative football career. My injury from that game kept me from ever playing again. He didn't do his job of protecting me on the field. I will never let him forget what he did to me. I have more money now than I would have ever made in football. What about Everly getting gone? Plans?"

Everly started to cry as she listened to them talk about her as if she was dirty gum on the bottom of their shoes. She was about to turn and run away when she was startled by a hand covering her mouth. Her eyes widened and then softened when Fancy, one of her father's three girlfriends pulled her back toward the steps and away from the balcony doors. When she started to fight her off, Fancy whispered that she was here to help her and not hurt her.

"I'm going to remove my hand. Please do not scream. In a few minutes, the guards will make their rounds. They will see you up here. Come with me," Fancy said against her ear.

Everly nodded and did what she was told. Following Fancy, they went down the stairs and headed back to Everly's room the same way that she'd exited it. Once inside, Fancy closed all of the curtains and left the room in complete darkness. Moving to the bathroom, the only place without a window, Fancy closed the door behind them.

"What's this?" Everly asked.

"You heard them. I know you did."

"They're going to kill me."

"That's the plan. That's always been the plan. Your father is as ruthless as they come. He gets what he wants and your man friend is just like him."

"He's not my friend. He coerced me. I didn't have a choice."

"I know the story. You had a choice. You chose the wrong one. I knew the minute you showed up here with Hamilton that you were not meant to ever leave here. You have a day, maybe two before you'll disappear, never to be seen again. I don't want that for you. I've seen your father disappear a lot of people over the years. He's a sociopath. I wish you had not come here. You have to leave!" Fancy declared with passion that told Everly that this was serious.

"I don't have anywhere to go. Hamilton has my passport. In fact, he has all of my identification. I don't know where he keeps it. Even if I left, the only place I know to go is back to the United States. I don't have anything. My signature is on everything when it comes to the ponzi scheme he and my father cooked up. I'm the attorney of record. Like they said, if anyone is coming, they are coming for me. I'll get arrested the minute I'm back on U.S. soil."

"I don't think so. At least I don't think it will happen right away."

"I've been so stupid," Everly bemoaned.

"They counted on you being naïve and you were. They knew using your brother and what he's been involved with that could land him in jail would get your cooperation."

"They watch me like a hawk. There is no way I could leave and get away."

"I'm going to help you."

"Why, Fancy? Why would you help me?"

"Because Arlo is a horrible man. It's taken me years to work on my own plan to escape his grasp. The things he's made me do. The things I've seen. I've been plotting a way out for a long time. He's been so focused on this latest money-making scam that I have been able to get some things worked out behind his back. One of those things has been getting your passport and identification away from Hamilton."

"What? How?"

"Everly, this isn't a time to play twenty questions. I was able to sneak your papers away from Hamilton and replace them with fake duplicates."

Everly watched Fancy take a black pouch out of an oversized brown bag that was slung over her shoulder. Fancy opened the pouch and poured out its contents. Everly couldn't believe her eyes. In front her were her passport, driver's license and her credit cards that Hamilton told her he was holding onto for safe keeping. There were also stacks of money in large bills."

"How did you get these?"

"Let's just say, I'm quite resilient. I've learned a lot from being under your father's thumb for the past five years. Tomorrow is your ticket for getting out of here. They don't suspect anything, especially when it comes to me. I'm going to tell Arlo that I need to go out shopping. He won't suspect anything because that's a norm for me. He keeps me happy and smiling by throwing money my way. They're also used to you going out with me. We'll do that tomorrow like we have done many times before. I have a friend who will get us both away from the security detail who will no doubt follow us."

"My sister? What about Ariel?"

Fancy smiled up at her thinking about the four-year-old daughter she has with Arlo.

"Don't worry about Ariel. I would never let anyone harm her. I need to get her way from your father. I've seen how he is with you and I don't want that for my daughter. I have a plan, though I can't say that you'll ever be able to see her again. When we disappear from here, I'm cutting all contact to any and every one I have ever known here. That's the only *way to keep her safe. The only way for you to be safe is to go back to the United States. Hamilton is too much of a punk to ever go back and face the consequences one day. Your father wouldn't dare. He's still on their radar for murder."*

"Murder? My father killed someone?" Everly asked.

She watched Fancy dart her attention away in order to not keep eye contact. Everly wondered what that was about.

"You really are green. I don't mean to be disrespectful, but you are clueless as to who your father is. I can't believe you couldn't see through who Hamilton was. They are the worst of the worst."

"My father. Who did he kill?" Everly demanded.

"Everly, I think it's best you don't know. You have enough to worry about once you get back home. Do you have anyone you can go to? Is that young man you told me about out of the question? You seem to still be in love with him."

"I never, ever stopped loving him. I hated having to make him think I didn't love him anymore. I did it to protect him. Hamilton made it clear that something horrible would not only happen to my brother, but to Carlos as well. I didn't know what to do. I had to go along with the plan he and my father put in place."

"I get it. I've been in this life quite a few years. I want a different life for me and Ariel. She deserves that. It will be a life of forever running away from your father, but I'll make it work. I'm doing what's best for her. You have to forget about what you've done and do what's best for you. Yes, that could mean prison if you go back. I can't tell you what to do. I was able to get you some really good fake identification so that you can get out of the country. If you go to the United States, I don't know how good it will work. They'll pass for

real in other countries. The choice is yours. I only wanted you to be able to get away from here. Take the chance when it comes. You have all of your identification you came here with along with the fake stuff. Don't act like anything is wrong; be normal and you should be okay. Maybe your friend can help you if you go back."

"I can't go back to Carlos after what I've done. I do have a friend in New York that I went to law school with. I can reach out to her when I get back until I can figure out what to do. I don't have a problem turning myself in. I've done wrong. I may have thought I was doing it for the right reasons, but it's still wrong. Most of what I allowed myself to be involved with didn't come to light until a few weeks ago. I'm surprised I haven't seen anything on the national news about it. That's odd."

"That's probably because they don't want you to know that they know. They are waiting for you to show back up thinking the coast was clear. Don't fall for it. If and when they find you if you go back, your name and face will be everywhere. Be ready for that."

"I will," Everly agreed.

"That's why you have to leave. I think they may suspect that you know. Let's sit down and talk about the plan for tomorrow. If it all goes well, you'll be on your way home. The minute we get to the airport, we're going in two different directions. We won't be able to communicate again. I do need one favor," Fancy said.

Fancy took her hands into hers and Everly held on tight.

"Anything," Everly replied quickly.

"Never, ever tell anyone about me or Ariel. When we disappear, we disappear. I will never speak of you again."

"I would never put you or my sister in jeopardy. I need a favor as well."

Fancy nodded.

"Who did my father kill?" Everly asked.

She waited through what appeared to be Fancy deciding if she was going to come clean or not. When their eyes locked once again, she knew she was about to get her answer.

"Your mother. Arlo killed your mother. She didn't leave you and your brother. Back then, he was a major crime boss in the Chicago area. Your mother was killed when she decided to blow the whistle on his illegal business. He killed her and made his way to South America where he has been all these years. Arlo left you and your brother and never looked back until he and Hamilton schemed to use you. I wish we had time for me to get into the background of all of that as well as how Hamilton was able to connect to your brother. Arlo is behind it all. Just know that you can't trust him or Hamilton ever again. Your one and only plan is to get out of here and never look back. Let's talk," Fancy said.

Everly joined her on the bathroom floor. She listened as Fancy laid everything out for her.

If it wasn't for the phone in her hotel suite snapping her back to the present, Everly would have been stuck on the actions of the following morning that finally led to her being free from Hamilton and Arlo, but in a lane to lose her freedom now that she was back home.

Stepping out of the shower, she raced to the phone and grabbed it before it could ring again.

"Hello?"

"Ms. Everly Robinson?" the female voice on the other end asked.

Hearing someone she didn't know say her name gave her pause. Who would be calling her. She decided to go with it to see where the conversation was going. If it was the authorities, it was time she walked that green mile and deal with the consequences.

"Yes. I'm Everly Robinson."

"My name is Nadine Wallington. I'm a white-collar criminal defense attorney who specializes in security exchange commission enforcement and other regulatory investigations including internal investigations, corporate governance, and criminal and civil litigation. I was retained to assist you with your case. Can we meet later today?" she asked.

Everly exhaled. For now, she was still safe.

"You were? How? Who retained you?" she asked.

"As far as I know, you have. If you're asking about the fee for retaining me, it's anonymous. I'm under the assumption that you are in need of a criminal defense attorney for some financial crimes you'll be charged with. If you agree to having me as your attorney, you will be charged in the next few days. We can't have you on the streets as a criminal avoiding the law. We will work to get you out for now. That may be hard since you were on the run for a while."

"That's true."

"Great. I don't know the full story."

"There is a lot," Everly admitted.

"I may be the only person who'll be able to get you through this with little to no jail time. How does that sound?" Nadine asked.

Everly started to cry. Things were happening for her. For the first time in a long time, what was happening wasn't all bad.

"Tell me when and where and I'll make my way there somehow."

"Don't worry about that. I'll come to you. I want to keep you out of the public eye until we have to put you there. First, let's talk so that I can get the full story from you in order to see if there is any way we can make some kind of deal. Does that work for you?"

Everly nodded her head furiously as tears flowed down her cheeks. She didn't know the chances of getting a break but if this lawyer could make it happen, she was all for it. She would share every bit of what she knew. There were also some papers that she didn't know she had that were given to her by Fancy, unbeknownst to her.

"Yes, that sounds perfect."

When the call ended, her body still dripping from the shower, she rushed back into the bathroom to towel herself dry. She looked at herself in the mirror before going back into the room and retrieving the one large suitcase she had traveled back to the states with. Pulling it out from the closet, she opened it and leafed through the stack of papers inside. They were copies of a lot of the documents she'd signed for her father and Hamilton. Fancy somehow was able to get the papers and then make copies. She's planted the suitcase in a locker at the airport. That was the first place they'd gone after getting away from Arlo's spies. They had gone to the airport that was furthest from Arlo's compound hoping that he and his men would assume they would go to one closer. Within an hour of slipping on a disguise, she was on her way home. Now she was here to play the waiting game of what would become her fate.

4

Joey tried his best to keep up with Carlos' quick, long strides across the parking garage. Though they exited the elevator together, before he could get three good steps out, Carlos was already a good three car lengths ahead of him. He smiled facetiously as he hustled to catch up to him. There was no doubt, Carlos was in a mood. Without a doubt, the reason for his foul mood was at the private bar at the casino having a good time with Alyssa and Marlow. That, he shook his head at, was Everly.

None of the ladies had been drinking. Still, even he had to admit, they were having the time of their lives listening to music, eating some good food and dancing. When Carlos stormed out, he knew his brother had reached his peak of being focused on Everly all evening. No one knew Carlos better than him. Carlos was still struggling with the fact that the woman he'd loved had shared herself with a man he'd called his best friend.

He and Hamilton had been staunch competitors against each other for as far back as he could remember to their high school days. With Everly, a line was cross that could never be erased or forgotten about. He hated this for Carlos. In spite of it all, he will always have his brother's back. That's why when Carlos stormed out of the casino bar, Joey followed him without hesitation. He was glad that Everly hadn't see them as they passed by on their way out. He saw the moment Carlos had caught a glimpse of Everly having fun as if she didn't have serious legal problems on the horizon.

Before leaving, Joey's eyes connected with Marlow's and without words, she understood. With a slight wave of her hand, she told him to go on and look after Carlos. The ride in the elevator was a quiet one. He didn't need to look at his brother to see he was troubled. They've always been each other's support. Nothing about that will ever change.

"Can you slow down a bit? You do realize you rode with me so I have the keys. You can't get in the car until I get there. Do you want to tell me what's happening in that pea brain of yours?" Joey kidded.

He was hoping to lighten Carlos' mood even a little.

"Walk faster," Carlos yelled over his shoulder after they had exited the elevator on the private level that required a card key or passcode to exit out of. "I've seen you move faster than this in the ring. I need to get out of here. I should have driven my own car," he further bemoaned.

"Well, why didn't you? Don't take my head off because you can't peel out of the parking lot on two wheels because you're pissed. Why are you still allowing what happened with Everly to get to you? I thought you were over her?"

"I am. What makes you think I'm not?"

They reached his car. Joey refused to unlock the car doors just yet.

"I saw you watching her tonight. Are you upset that she's not in the slumps anymore? I mean, yeah, she still has this legal issue hanging over her head. In the midst of that, she was able to shed angst over what she's going through. She had on her happy face tonight. For the first time in over a week, she's smiling, according to Marlow. You, on the other hand, spent the entire night looking like someone just killed your dog. Then when you saw her, it was like you had just had the burial at the pet cemetery. Why are you acting bothered if you're really unbothered?"

Carlos leaned on the car with both hands flat on the hood.

"You saw her. She's acting like what happened with us didn't happen. She's smiling, laughing and dancing around like she doesn't have a care in the world. She could go to prison. Maybe that hasn't set in for her yet. She could go away for a long time if she loses her court case. All that drama we went through for her to end up back here penniless, husbandless and friendless."

"No. Now, she's not friendless. She has all of us. Aren't you happy knowing that she was never married to Hamilton? That was all a lie on his part? He wanted to get under your skin and it's clear that he still is."

Carlos turned sharply in his direction. Joey knew he'd said the wrong words for Carlos' ears but they were still true nonetheless.

"Right. She shows back up and everyone is taking pity on her. She's like best friends with Marlow and Alyssa now. Now she's back like nothing happened."

"That bothers you? Something did happen. She also met with her lawyer a few days ago. Mind you, it's the lawyer you are paying for, but we're still not telling anybody. The bar was closed so there was no risk to anyone seeing her. That's why they were there. Everly has been in that suite since she got here. In two days, she'll be turning herself in and facing the charges that her lawyer, Nadine said she was able to get information about from the FBI. It was okay for her to have a moment of happiness."

Joey leaned on the car next to Carlos.

"It doesn't bother you that she's here? That I'm helping her without her knowing it's me?" Carlos asked.

"No, it doesn't. Look, I'm not one for holding grudges. That's not who I am. Besides, when she showed up here, you were the one asking all of us to help her. Our sister and friends are doing that. Everly doesn't have anyone. She needs a circle around her. Have you tried talking to her about what happened?"

Joey leaned to the side with Carlos' anger had daggers shooting out of his eyes on that question.

"What is there to say?"

"So, when you're around her, nothing is said about the past?"

"No. I don't want to bring that old stuff back up. There's no need to. We haven't talked at all."

"Really? You know that for a fact? What if I told you that there is more to the story than what you think you know? What if you could finally get closure for what happened before? It's clear you haven't moved beyond it. Do you know what else is clear?"

Joey crossed his arms and his legs and waited. When he didn't say anything else, he got the reaction he was expecting from Carlos. The annoyed look on his face said it all.

"Tell me or shut up about it!" Carlos yelled and shoved him lightly.

"You may be the bigger brother, but you and I both know I can take you down in less than sixty seconds. Push me again and find out."

"Out with it. You seem to know it all. I guess you fixed your own life and you think that makes you some kind of an expert on everyone else's."

Carlos huffed loudly. Joey shook his head from side to side. His brother really was clueless.

"I know you're still in love with Everly."

The loud pitch of Carlos' sudden laughed shocked Joey. He wasn't expecting that.

"What are you smoking, bro? Does Marlow know? It must be something good because you are insane. I'm not in love with Everly anymore. That thing is dead, buried and stinking. I'm over it."

"Maybe so. You're not over her though. Anyway, we could go back and forth about this all day. I'm saying, talk to her. I think there are some things you need to know that only Everly can make clear."

"Oh? And how do you know so much?"

"Man, there are so many secrets and lies mixed all up in the story of Carlos and Everly. I won't even include Hamilton because he's not worth the air he breathes. I know that sounds childish but I'm working on cleaning up my language. What I'd really like to say and the way I want to say it could keep me from getting into heaven someday, so I digress. I've worked hard to cut a lot of cursing out of my vocabulary. I have some colorful words I could use to describe him but I won't. I'll stick with calling him a punk because he left a woman in a lurch to take his case for him."

"What does that mean?"

"Carlos, I'm not going to do this with you. I came out behind you because I saw the look on your face in the way you couldn't tear your eyes away from Everly."

"Did she see me?"

"I don't know. Marlow saw me because I sent her a text to let her know we were in the corner by the door. I made it known you were with me and that we didn't want to interrupt their ladies night out where they had the entire bar to themselves thanks to Torrence. There are a few hours left before that location is open to the public for the night. She thought I was home in bed waiting on her. She knows I've been in meetings all day with my agent."

"Did she say anything to Everly about me being there?"

"No, she didn't tell Everly you were here stalking her from a dark corner," he joked.

"Give it a rest, bro. I wanted to see how she was doing. I got my answer. Now I can leave. Can you take me back to my car, please? We look odd having this chat in the garage without getting in the car."

"Only the security team can see us in the cameras and they don't care. Not until you tell me that you're going to talk to Everly."

"What do you know? This is more than just me talking to her."

"I wouldn't usually keep anything from you but I promised Marlow."

"She knows? They just met and she knows? What the hell!"

"I don't think it's that deep. From what Marlow says, Everly only mentioned that everything isn't what it really appeared to be. Her issue is, she doesn't know if you would ever want to hear her truth after all this time."

"I was there for her truth. If it walks like a duck and talks like a duck...You know the rest. Can we leave now?"

Carlos walked around to the passenger side door and pulled the handle. Nothing happened. Joey chuckled when he tested Carlos' patience by unlocking and locking the door back when Carlos tried to open it.

"I'm going to need a better mood from you first," Joey said.

"I can always call a rideshare. I'm never stranded."

"Oh, please. You can't stand being in the passenger seat of my car. I cannot picture you being in the back seat of a stranger's car. Try that with someone else. Look, I'm only saying I don't like to see you like this. Remember my struggles with Marlow? You were all over me not messing up a good thing with her."

"Because you were in love with her?"

"And you're not?"

"What? Not in love with Marlow? Bro, we don't hang like that!"

When Carlos laughed to the point that his whole body vibrate, Joey didn't even mind the lame joke. He was happy that Carlos was laughing and smiling.

"Whatever. You know what I mean. Even if you're not in love with her, you should still talk to her and clear the air. It would be good for both of you. I know one thing, Alyssa told me that this lawyer of hers is top-tier. I know you paid the retainer. It's wild to hear that she's taking the case pro-bono. This will be a big, high-profile case. Probably the biggest Chicago has ever seen. I'm surprised she's representing her for free."

"Yeah, I got a check back for the retainer you paid from my account. I put it in the bank earlier today," Carlos noted.

"Apparently, Reese's marketing firm was able to get her some big promos for one of the most powerful law firms in Chicago. Clients were banging down the door after Reese re-tooled the marketing strategy. Besides, I hear that Everly is being railroaded because she's an attorney. She's being made an example of to show that lawyers are not above the law."

"Well, I wouldn't know. I'm trying to stay out of it. I'm happy she's got a nice network around her."

"Talk to her, Carlos. I think the revelations will bring the relief from what happened that you haven't been able to get. Everly needs to unload a lot; unpack a lot. She should only do that with you."

"I don't know. There was a lot that was left unsettled. She walked out like it was nothing. We were in something deep and intense. We loved hard. Her betrayal can't have an explanation. Hamilton. It was Hamilton! I've been hesitant about having friendships like that again. I can't even think about a serious relationship with anyone. Hamilton, dude. It was that clown! I know we competed in every aspect of life, but I also thought we were friends."

"I get it. He walked away with your woman. Neither of them ever looked back. Don't you want to know why?"

"I know why."

"No, you don't. I don't know either, but according to Marlow, there is so much more to the story than what you know. Let's get out of here," Joey said unlocking the doors as they got in.

"It's early. You're going home? Looks like your woman will be a while? You sure you don't want to wait for her?"

"No. Alyssa will bring her home. She sent me a text that she'll be home in an hour. She's off tomorrow. We plan on making it a marathon of love making for the next two days. I'm going home to set a romantic mood for my baby."

"I like that," Carlos acknowledged. He truly loved Marlow for his brother. "From the woman who caused your major car accident that could have been fatal, to being your physical therapist to now being the love of your life? Your life is the kind of stuff Hallmark movies are made of," he added.

Joey started the car and pulled out of the parking space.

"I am the luckiest brother on this planet because of how perfect Marlow is for me. At one time, that was you and Everly. I'm not saying you'll ever get back to that. There is a lot that was left undone and unsaid. Close it out so that you can move on. You have a major chip on your shoulder whenever her name comes up. Talk to her and shake it off."

Carlos nodded and reached for the button to the satellite radio. Changing the station, a *WuTang Clan* song blasted through the speakers. Carlos turned the volume on high, leaned back and closed his eyes. Joey knew the conversation was over.

5

"Are you watching this?"

Carlos looked up from his spot in the center of the casino main security office after hearing Melvin's voice. From where he loved to sit and keep an eye on things, he could see all eighty security cameras that spanned all four of the room walls. The twelve security specialists whose only jobs were to watch the cameras around the clock to note anything suspicious. None of them budged or looked up when Melvin entered the room to address him. Carlos' crooked smile was a sign that the team had been trained well. They were never to be distracted by anything when it came to watching the cameras they are assigned to.

"It's happening now?" Carlos asked.

He knew what Melvin was referencing. He'd asked his head of security to let him know the minute he saw anything on the news. Apparently, Everly's time had come.

Carlos spent the morning avoiding his sister knowing that Alyssa wanted to know how he was handling not only having Everly back in town for the past two weeks at the same hotel that he called home but also knowing that the night before, she'd finally been arrested after she and her attorney walked her into the local FBI office. Thankfully, it didn't happen publicly at the hotel. Instead, her new attorney was able to allow Everly to turn herself in at night, under the cover of darkness. Soon after, her arrest had been leaked to the press. Journalist from all over were able to make it to Chicago by early morning in order to capture Everly being escorted into the courthouse knowing her charges were going to be read.

"Yes. It's not easy to watch either. I didn't realize how many people are out to see her taken down. The crowd is massive," Melvin said.

Carlos stood quickly. His chair toppled to the floor. No doubt, the lines across his forehead were sharp and filled with the anger he was feeling boiling over.

"I thought they were going to let her be released after court in a private manner as not to expose her to public scrutiny. Chicago and all of those impacted by what happened were certainly going to be out in crowds. They had to know it would be a circus."

"I don't know what happened because what I see is definitely a circus and very public," Melvin explained.

Carlos took his phone out and rushed out of the office. He logged his phone into his favorite national television app knowing that the news wasn't just local news. He walked into his private office through the door right next to the security booth. No one was there. Melvin followed him inside and closed the door behind them. Without saying anything else, Carlos watched in horror as microphones from every news station were shoved into Everly's face as she and Nadine left federal courthouse. He'd never seen so many people trying to get close to someone for a news story. He tried watching the news the evening before when word had leaked out about Everly being back in Chicago and why there was such interest in her. It was painful to hear the stories of why she was being charged. The years she could spend in prison was too much to bear. Who was this woman he once loved? He couldn't believe what the full story was that had now come out. Every detail had been leaked to the press.

Leaning against his desk, he watched in horror as someone in the crowd hurdled raw eggs at Everly, hitting her square in the face. The words from an angry mob were the most atrocious, vile descriptions of a person that he'd ever heard.

"Why isn't she better protected? Look at that mob! What the hell?" Carlos yelled at his phone.

"I know. It's crazy," Melvin agreed.

Before he could say another word, there was a shift in the crowd. After a lot of shoving, not only did those in the media get shoved to the ground, but so did Everly, her attorney and the few federal officers who faked protecting them from the mob.

Once on the ground, he watched as Everly tried to stand while covering her face. Her attorney tried to help along with, what appeared to be a few other lawyers with her, but their attempts were not successful. Mayhem ensued. There was yelling, screaming and a bunch of people trying to grab for Everly. They looked like they wanted to tear her apart.

Carlos' anger went over the top. He slammed his fist on his desk and growled. That was the moment that he knew he should have been there. He'd spent the better part of the week avoiding any interaction with Everly at the hotel. Outside of a few visits to her lawyer's office, she hadn't left the casino hotel. Being out wasn't going to be good for her. Thankfully, to get into the casino and the hotel, all visitors had to get through one of four security gates. Everyone was scrutinized on a regular day. Somehow, the media had yet to discover where Everly was staying. He knew that would soon change now that everything regarding Everly being in Chicago was out in the open. He had to do something. She was practically being trampled.

"Speak to the team about the potential of having media and unwanted visitors outside of the gates trying to get to Everly once they find out she's staying here. Make sure there is a plan in place to protect the casino and Everly. I don't want what we see on the screen to happen here at the casino," he said to Melvin.

"I'm already on it. I'm bringing on a few guys for extra shifts. We're already getting them rooms so that they can get long breaks without having to leave. There are two wedding receptions here this weekend. We're ready for that as well. We have the list of visitors for that. The team is ready," Melvin explained.

Carlos was kicking himself. He was so angry that he couldn't see ahead of what could have and is happening.

"I should have been there. Look at that. Why aren't the police doing anything? They're just standing around," he yelled angrily. "I think a few of them are laughing!"

"Boss, you can't be everywhere."

"True. I could have been there. I knew what was going to happen. I've been in security a long time. We've seen this before with Madoff. Remember that story? I still remember the footage of him after he was released and able to go home. He was followed and taunted every step of the way. Everly can't handle this. She's not that strong."

Carlos could see her crying as cameras were focused on her on the ground. He wanted to hit someone; *anyone*. It's true she was not his responsibility but she had no one. He had to convince his sister and Marlow to not go to the courthouse to support Everly today. He knew what could happen and it did. He protected them but not Everly.

"Listen, you know we can help her. All you have to do is say the word. I'll be all over it. I can have guys on her like a second skin every time she leaves out. I'm surprised the judge let her out. That must have been one hell of a fight her lawyer put up."

Carlos nodded in agreement. He was thinking the same thing. He'd been concerned all morning that after being locked up last night, the judge would issue a no-bail for her to be sure she wouldn't skip town. Something miraculous must have happened. He listened to one reporter, who had been in the courtroom, say that she granted Everly's release after she turned over her passport. Her bail was set at one million dollars cash.

"With a bail that high, I can't believe she's out."

Melvin looked over at him quizzically.

"You didn't pay it?"

Carlos had it, but no, he didn't pay it. He would have had to pull all of his financial resources together to come up with that amount in cash. He had no idea who paid it. Someone had. He wanted to know who did.

"No. I paid the retainer which was returned to me. Apparently after talking with Everly, she believed her. She's not confident she can get her completely off, but she wants the chance to try. This would be the biggest case of her career. Not to mention, if she wins, the amount of work that will come into the firm she works for will raise the bar for them in the legal world. Her bail is a different story. I can't imagine who else she knows who has a million dollars in cash laying around."

Carlos gasped when he saw Everly fall to the ground a second time after she was pushed right before getting into the black Expedition truck at the curb of the courthouse. Another wave of shoving sent her flying head first into the truck before she collapsed. One of Chicago's best finally did step up to help by picking Everly up. He lifted her into the truck and closed the door. The truck sped away and entered traffic before it disappeared out of sight of every camera.

"Boss?" Melvin asked.

"Yeah."

Carlos still had his eyes on the news. He couldn't believe how much worse the situation could have been. There were people in that crowd who had murder in their eyes.

"Well?"

Carlos turned his attention to Melvin.

"Well, what?"

"Are we going to help? She'll have a lot of days in court. She'll need to get back and forth to her lawyer's office. Her face will be recognized by everyone after today. She won't be able to hide out for long."

Carlos sat against the table with his legs spread wide and firmly planted on the floor. His hands again grasped the edge of the desk.

"One female and two males. At least one of them with her at all times except when she's in her hotel suite. Let's have another on watch and out of sight but close enough to see everything around her. He can warn of any aggression."

"What if any cars are following them to try and find where she is whenever she's out and about?" Melvin asked.

Carlos didn't answer. He took out his phone and called Everly's attorney. He had added her number to his phone just in case he needed to reach her after Joey paid the retainer from his account. No one needed to know that, except Melvin who saw him hit one number.

"Nadine Wallington."

Carlos dived right in.

"Nadine? This is Carlos. I was watching the news. Are you both alright?" he asked.

"Yes. Everly is shook up but she's fine."

"Where are you headed?"

"My office. She needs a cooling off period. I also have a lot to go over with her."

"How are you getting her back to the hotel?"

"I haven't thought about that yet."

"Tell me, is there a garage that you park in when you're at your office? What's that situation look like? Is it public or private?"

Carlos shot one question after another at her. He was hyped up and ready to leap into action. Protecting Everly was on the top of his list.

"It's a public garage. Our level uses a cardkey to enter our four floors."

Carlos' mind was going a million miles a minute. Eventually, Everly needed to get out of there without being seen. He had to prepare himself and his team for what they do best. They operate in wild situations.

"Okay, listen to me closely. When it's time to leave, I have no doubt the media will be all around. Can you get Everly to another floor in your building that leads to the garage?"

"Yes. I can do that. She'll still be recognized now that an updated image of her is available."

"I'm going to send a woman from my team to impersonate her. She'll have a wig and other attire for Everly. Have them switch places. By the time the media find out it's not Everly in the truck, she'll be in another vehicle on her way to the hotel. No one can get in here without going through security. Keep her there at least two hours. My team is on the way. We'll provide protection from here on out."

"Thank you. I was telling Everly that her safety will be at risk throughout this process."

"That may be true in some instances. For this time right now, under my watch, it won't be possible. I'll be in touch," he said.

"Would you like to talk to Everly? She's right here next to me."

Carlos hesitated and then knew that now wasn't the time.

"Not right now. I have things to put in place," he said.

Before Nadine could say anything else, he disconnected the call and placed his phone back in his pocket. He looked to Melvin. When he headed toward the office door, Carlos knew that no words were needed. Melvin knew what to do.

~~

"Damn! Everly is going to tell everything."

Hamilton paced around the bungalow that he had been staying in the moment he realized over a week ago that Everly was gone. She and Fancy left Arlo's compound to go shopping and never returned. Arlo searched high and low for the women and his daughter and found nothing. No one was talking. Hamilton remembered hearing about them not returning and raced to his own room to check the safe. There was no way Everly could have figured out the combination. On the other hand, reality had hit him like a ton of bricks. This was Arlo's place and Fancy played innocent and naïve but he caught on right away after meeting her that there was more to her than what met the eye.

Before he had even opened the door to the safe, he knew that Everly and Fancy had been in cahoots. They were always huddled up. When they were caught, they would giggle as if they weren't talking about anything too deep. Women were scandalous. That's why he never committed himself to any woman. They couldn't be trusted. Before he could pick up his phone to call Arlo, it rang and the man's name was on the screen.

"What the hell, Hamilton? Did you hear?" Arlo asked, screaming so loud that Hamilton moved the phone away from his ear.

"I, not only heard, I also saw it on the internet. The FBI? The SEC? She's going to bury us! Why would she go back? That was a stupid move on her part," Hamilton screamed.

"Do something. You were supposed to keep her in check," Arlo shouted.

"She's your daughter!" Hamilton countered.

"You're going back to the states, right? I would join you but I need to find Fancy and my daughter. I wouldn't care if it wasn't for the fact she stole a bucketload of money from me. She left and took my daughter, the only one of my kids who mean anything to me. I'm leaving here. There's no telling how much she's already told them. You had better do something about her. Do it now, Hamilton."

"Hold up! Why don't you do something about her?"

"This is on you. She can bury you and your father's company. She's served her purpose. You set for your return?" Arlo asked.

Hamilton looked to his luggage already packed. He looked in the mirror at his new appearance. That along with the fake identification that had no doubt been the route Everly had also taken to leave the country, was how he was escaping. He was sure he'd have no problem slipping back into the United States undetected. He had already done it several times since leaving almost a year ago. He had to figure out a way to get to Everly before she was able to tell her story in court. From the news, her first court date had only been set to lay out the charges. She wasn't set to testify or tell the story yet. He had to get to her before she did that.

What Everly had to say would not only take him down, but his entire family. He and his father didn't have the best of a relationship. There was a lot riding on getting to Everly. Arlo was right. She was his to take care of. It was he who brought her into the fold, unknowingly. If he could slip back into the states, he certainly could sidle up to Everly when she least expected it. If he was as smart as he knew he was, he knew exactly where to find her. Everly went back to Carlos. They wouldn't be expecting him.

"I'm all set. I'll take care of her. You handle what you need to handle. I'll be in and out of that country within days, I'm sure. Everly has taken her last flight, that's for sure," Hamilton exclaimed with assurance.

After listening to Arlo cheering on the other end, Hamilton hung up. He grabbed is things and headed for the airport. He knew he would emerge victorious, rich and no longer out for revenge.

After months of Everly denying him her sexy body, he looked forward to finally getting his hands on her and getting what he is owed before his hands snuffed the life out of her. She was what stood between him and a life of money, leisure and happiness in a part of the world where he'd never be found again. He was ready. This, he knew, was the only way. His only regret was not taking care of her right after the money was safely in his hands.

6

Everly found herself in seclusion. Life was coming at her hard. She didn't see a happy way out of it at this point. A few days ago, she played cloak and dagger just to get back to the suite that protected her from the outside world where it seems people were out for her blood.

After getting a hot bath that lasted over an hour, she slipped into some yoga pants and a tank top. She ordered room service which was still sitting on a tray hear the door. Under the domes were a chicken salad sandwich, a bowl of fresh fruit, and two brownies, her weakness. Until today, everything she had was at someone else's expense.

Not only had Nadine been working hard on her court case, she'd also secured the money from a trust fund that had been set up for her by her mother when she was a child. No doubt the money had come from her father's ill-gotten gained riches. There was also additional money added to her trust fund from a lawsuit filed against the city of Chicago on behalf of her and her brother after they were assaulted while under the watchful eye of the department of child services.

The only money that Everly remembered taking from her trust fund was for college and for the house that she'd bought and eventually sold to Joey when she decided to move in with

Carlos. Living together had only lasted a few months before all hell broke loose.

Her trust fund was safe and secure from any seizure or confiscation by the government. The hold that had been placed on that account was released to her earlier in the day. The amount wouldn't set her up for life, but it would help her to survive. She could also pay for her stay at the casino and every meal that so far had been given to her. At first, Torrence wouldn't allow her to pay. After thanking him for his kindness, she asked to be able to pay at least half. With that and the large tipping she did for the staff who assisted her, she felt better about not taking advantage of anyone. She even offered to pay her attorney. Nadine still wouldn't take anything from her.

Moving to the window that overlooked the Chicago skyline, she looked out over the city that she loved. The sight was beautiful. She missed it the minute she'd stepped on a plane to leave the country. If she could have thought of another choice, she would have made it. Leaving, not just Chicago, but Carlos was the biggest mistake of her life. She was happy to be home while at the same time, depression was setting in. This wasn't only due to the case, but to the fact that it was obvious Carlos was avoiding her. She's spent time with his sister and their friends, but each time, he was ghost. She'd hurt him, that was a surety. She wondered if he would ever give her the chance to come clean about everything. It won't get her back to a life with him, but at least, she could free his mind over what he thought happened but never had.

There were only a few people who now knew her truth. She'd told most of what happened to her to Alyssa and Marlow over the days after her return. She couldn't hold it in any longer considering Carlos wouldn't talk to her. The fact that

Alyssa treated her kindly before hearing the story was a testament to the great people she and her brothers are.

The only others who knew her story were her two best friends, Cecily and Nola Fredericks. Only Nola lived in Chicago. They had been her link to life since they were college roommates.

After news of her arrest broke, she had reached out to Nola who welcomed her with open arms. She hadn't seen her yet but that would be changing soon. She still hadn't had a chance to connect with Cecily, to her chagrin. She would continue to try and reach her to explain everything.

Even though Nola offered to let her camp out at her house, she didn't want to involve her friend into her drama. How she could allow herself to be swindled into doing something she knew was wrong she didn't know.

Looking out at the bright lights of the city, the view reminded her of trip she'd taken to Las Vegas for one of Carlos and Joey's wrestling matches. They had stayed at the Aria, her favorite Las Vegas hotel. She was surprised to hear that he'd given up that career to focus full-time on their private security business. He'd been doing that along with wrestling throughout their relationship. Though Joey lived and loved wrestling, Carlos enjoyed being in that business with his brother, though it wasn't his first love.

The biggest change in Carlos was his hair. When they were dating, he loved sporting sexy braids. The fact that he was now bald, was a welcomed surprise. When she saw him, her mind went back to the romantically, desirable days and nights of their love. She missed that. She missed him. Being in the city that they both loved reminded her of the life she allowed to slip through her fingers. There it was again; regret.

On the nightstand, the cellphone she was able to purchase earlier pinged. She left her seat at the window and reached for it. Only a few people had the number. One of those people was Nola. The call had to be her. Alyssa and Marlow were busy with their husbands tonight. Carlos also had the number but she didn't suspect he would use it. He hadn't even come by to see her since she's been here. Nadine was the last person she'd shared the number with. They didn't have another meeting for a few days while they were in the discovery phase.

"Hello?"

"Hey girl!" Nola said with exuberance.

"Hey yourself. You're my first call. I thought you were my lawyer, then I realized how late it was in the evening. How are you?"

"I was calling to ask you the same thing. I love that you finally have a phone. I hated having to call the hotel to speak to you. I've never been that scrutinized in my life! It was all good though. I know they were looking out for your safety. Once, I forgot to use the fake name you gave me. When I said your name, they immediately said no one was there under that name and hung up on me."

"I know. That was a pain. Once my trust fund was released back to me, a cellphone was my first purchase. Now, you can call me directly. I haven't had much money since I got here other than what I brought with me from South America. I told you about how Fancy gave me some money. Thanks also for the money you sent me. I'm taking money out of the trust to pay you back."

"You'll do nothing like that. I gave you that because I love you."

"Despite what I did turning my back on everyone?" Everly asked.

"I understand why; I get it. Have you told the story to you know who?"

"No. He hasn't really talked to me."

"Didn't you say he lived at the casino in one of the suites?"

"He does, but I haven't seen him other than in passing. He's orchestrating my security when I need to leave the hotel to see my lawyer or go to court."

"It's not him?"

"Girl, no. Carlos hates me too much to be security for me. I can see it in his eyes. Are you still coming to see me?"

"I am. I'm actually here now, earlier than I thought. Trae is at home with the kids tonight so that I could come see you. I was going to wait until they were in bed, but he hustled me out saying he could handle them. I'm imagining toys and everything else being all over the place when I get home," she laughed.

"You're here?"

"Yes. If you open the door, I'm five steps from your door. If I thought calling to talk to you was hard, you should have seen the hoops I had to go through to see you. If it wasn't for Carlos adding me to a list to come see you, I would have been out of luck. You know me. Either way, I would have come up with some story to get me here to you."

"I'll have to thank him for that one day when he is talking to me again," Everly said as she rushed to the door and opened it. She jumped up and down the moment she saw Nola standing on the other side with her arms open wide.

"Why didn't you start the conversation with you being here already? Come on in here. We need to order you something to eat. I thought you were coming by later so I only order a light snack for myself."

"Oh?" What did you get?" Nola asked, walking over to the food cart to lift the silver lids. Without saying anything, Nola grabbed a handful of grapes before checking out the suite.

"No need for me to answer that now, I guess," she chuckled while pointing to the three grapes Nola shoved in her mouth.

"I'm starving. I'm thinking a burger, fries, milkshake and some kind of pie," Nola said plopping down on the bed.

"That I can do."

Everly reached for the electronic pad and started ordering a bunch of food for them.

"Say, what about your brother? Any word on him since you returned?" Nola asked.

"Despite Hamilton's promise that he wouldn't touch my brother with his threats, while I was in South America, he had Dante arrested. He somehow leaked information to the authorities here about the smuggling ring my brother was involved in. He's in custody and on his way to doing six years in prison. He was caught up in some kind of sting at the Port of Chicago where young women were being smuggled in from South America. He was involved with something Hamilton roped him into. Hamilton got his money, but my brother was caught with a crazy amount of fentanyl along with the girls. After all of my drama is over, hopefully successfully, I hope to focus on getting my brother a better attorney. I will say, he was caught with enough for him to get no bail. Imagine that. My brother and I both in trouble with the law."

"You're out though. Why isn't he?" Nola asked.

"The way the law works, I guess. Nadine has managed to convince the court that there is more to the story. I plan to tell them all that I know. Hamilton is out of the country. He wouldn't dare come back here. He can't threaten me, Carlos or my brother anymore. I want this over with so that I can get back to some type of life."

"A life with Carlos?"

"I doubt it."

"Tell him."

"I can't. He won't believe me."

"You won't know unless you tell him, right? Are you going to at least try?"

Everly finished the order and fell onto the bed near the top. She grabbed a pillow and propped it up under her head.

"You get that I understand his anger, right? I mean, I look at what it would feel like if the tables were turned. I don't know if I would have ever recovered. You should have seen his eyes when he first saw me. I wasn't expecting compassion, trust me. I didn't expect to see hate. I've never seen that in his eyes before. Even with that, I put my pride aside and asked for his help. Without hesitation, he gave that."

"That's because he's an amazing man. Should I also say, he may have feelings for you even now."

"I don't think that's possible. Imagine him thinking I have been intimate with his best friend; or a man he thought was his best friend but never really was. Hamilton has always competed with Carlos. I didn't know that. I thought it was friendly rivalry. I was the one thing in Carlos' life that Hamilton wanted to conquer to be able to say that he had finally beat Carlos at something in life. There's a whole story there that I can't go into right now. I want to have a light evening tonight; nothing too heavy on my heart. I will figure things out with Carlos. How long are you staying tonight?"

"I'm hoping long enough to go to one of the clubs downstairs."

Everly looked at her sideways.

"This face is recognizable now. I can't do that," Everly explained.

"You have been in this room too long. You need to be around people."

The idea made her nervous. She'd been given strict instructions from her attorney to keep a low profile until everything was over. Going to a club could cause another scene like the one at the courthouse. That experience was one she never wanted to live through again.

"No way, Nola. We can catch up right here in this room. Besides, the food should be here any minute."

"Chick, it's only seven in the evening. The night is young. If you look in the bag I brought with me, you will see some good stuff that I think will aid you in being out in public tonight and for the foreseeable future. Are you game?"

Everly smiled and raced for the bag that Nola dropped at the door. She quickly rummaged around inside and shrieked with excitement. Inside she found a sexy chestnut wig with blond highlights. There were some sexy diamond-crusted eye glasses, she was assuming were non-prescription. There were several sexy dresses for both of them to choose from. Included was also a pair of black and diamond strappy stilettos, just her type of shoe.

"Nola!" she shouted. "What have you done?"

"I've created a way for you to move out and about. For the daytime, there are some sunglasses inside. That's a start to the wigs. You know I'm the wig queen. Not all of us have perfect hair, a mixture of Spanish and American heritage in our blood. With the perfect makeup, you will go so incognito that you won't even recognize yourself if you pass by a mirror. I hear Jill Scott is performing tonight as a favor to the owner who I understand has some roots in Philly? I know you want to hear her. You love her music and so do I. I think this will work."

Everly looked from the clothes to Nola and then back to the clothes. She wondered if she could pull it off. Was it really worth the risk? She was getting claustrophobic sitting in this room day and night. She truly was going stir-crazy. Her friend was here for the rescue.

"This could be a disaster, Nola."

"It could be. It could also be fun. If you put that wig and glasses on, no one will know it's you. Let's have a little fun for a little while. Let's step you out of this crazy reality and into something that will help put a smile on your face. I know of something or should I say someone else, but you won't even try. In place of that kind of fun, let's do this. At the first sign of any issues, we are out of there. We can even stay in the back where it will be darker. Come on. Say you will?"

As Nola continued to plead, Everly held the little black dress up to her shapely body and imagined herself in it. Could she really? She had to think about some things. Then she realized, but not tonight.

"Let's do it!" she shouted.

That got a rise and a celebratory dance out of Nola. Deciding to join in the fun, Everly grabbed her phone and put some music on as they danced around the room. She loved dancing. At the moment, she felt freer than she had in a long time.

7

"Carlos? Did you hear me?"

Ayanna Denton had waited a long time to be asked out by Carlos. His company had provided security for her father, an African prince, who had been in Chicago for a meeting with city and state officials on discussions about joint business ventures. He hadn't been the one providing the extra security her father needed, but he'd put his team in place. She was able to meet him on her father's last day in the country. She'd returned in the past few days because she loved Chicago for the time she'd been here. Also, she couldn't stop thinking about Carlos.

When he invited her to hear Jill Scott in concert, she jumped at the chance to spend some time with him. Tonight, she was hoping for more than just a concert. The man was a walking delicacy. She smiled when he turned toward her in the booth they sat in as they enjoyed Jill's sultry voice.

"What? Oh, I'm sorry," Carlos said.

"You can't blame it on the music. You were only here physically. Where is your mind? I hope it's on me," Ayanna said, looping her arm around his, leaning closer into him so that he could hear her. She'd been talking to him and had not gotten a response.

"As beautiful as you are, how could I be thinking of anything else?"

"That's what I like to hear. I thought you showing me around Chicago today was great. Tonight is amazing. I know you are a busy man. I pulled you away from work."

"You were well worth it."

Ayanna kissed him on the side of his lips.

"You made last night worth my trip here. Thanks for the most amazing sleepover I've ever had in my life. I'm sure you don't need to be told how masterful you are when it comes to knowing your way around a woman's body. I wish I wasn't flying out early in the morning or I'd stay another night. As it is, I still need to pack. My escort is expecting me back at my hotel tonight," she explained.

Carlos kissed her sweetly on the lips.

"Well, I'm glad your escort had no problem with you spending the night with me last night. I know how your father is about, well, what we did last night. He's very protective of you and your image."

"That he is. I will say, he likes you. You emit so much power and strength. Not to mention you are serious about your business. My father respects that in any man. I must say, I very much enjoyed your power and your strength last night," she whispered close to his ear.

Carlos was about to respond when the host took to the microphone on the stage to announce that Jill Scott was taking a thirty-minute break. The DJ who opened the show would fill in with playing music until she returned. This was his time to focus on Ayanna. He didn't want to share that his mind was elsewhere tonight. Even though he and Everly were not an item, he couldn't stop thinking about her.

He tried getting her off of his mind by hanging out and in with Ayanna. They had fun, but it didn't work. He loved sex and Ayanna helped him scratch an itch. They agreed it was non-committal fun but he was getting the feeling she was seeing more in what they shared than what he did. For that, if it were the case, he was sorry.

"Your father is a great and highly respected man. We had a good talk when he was here. He gave me some business advice that will take me a long way. I understand he's coming back to the states in a few months. To New York this time?"

"He is. I'm hoping he'll let me tag along. Do you think we can connect while he's here? I can get to Chicago if you can't make it to New York."

"I can't make a promise, but I'll let you know. Work is ramping up."

"Believe me, I know. You have the same work ethic as my father. While Jill is taking her break, tell me what makes you happy. What makes you smile besides amazing sex?"

Carlos was taking a gulp of his beer when her comment sent some liquid the wrong way. He choked slightly at her bluntness. He loved a woman who spoke her mind. Their night of sex the evening before was filled with a lot of blunt statements about what she enjoyed doing to him. They did have a night filled with sexiness. He hadn't planned on it, but should have expected it when he invited her to his suite. Her acceptance came out without any hesitation.

When he told her what he had in mind, she was all in. The moment they were inside of his suite, he picked her up and they went straight to the bedroom. Hours later, they emerged for sustenance because the sex had been wild. It wasn't that he didn't like his intimacy that way, he hated that it was an act of fulfillment for him. He felt no emotions when it came to her. He liked Ayanna a lot. Under any other circumstances, he would have given her the more that he knew she was looking for. Since Everly's return, he was tossed about what he wanted in a woman. He wasn't ready for anything other than a casual romp in the sheets. They did that. He knew tonight was her last night so he invited her to the concert as a send-off. Now, he was hearing her make plans for them to connect again and that worried him.

He was about to let her down easy, as he should have the day before but didn't because he physically desired her, when he felt a tap on his shoulder. It was Alyssa.

"Hey Car!" she exclaimed and pulled him up into a hug.

"What are you doing here? I wasn't expecting you. Is Dexter with you?" he asked.

"He's at a table closer to the stage. We decided to check this out before our trip tomorrow."

"You're still going to Los Angeles for that wedding? I thought you were thinking of staying home because of the boys?"

When Alyssa's eyes darted to his left, he remembered Ayanna was sitting at the table.

"Hello," Ayanna said, speaking up first.

"Sorry about that. This is Ayanna. She's a friend in town."

Carlos moved to the side when Ayanna extended her hand.

"It's nice to meet you," she said to Alyssa. "You're very beautiful. I'm sure you already know that," she added.

"The feeling is mutual. I don't mean to interrupt. I asked one of his men if he was working tonight and I was told he was back here. They didn't say he was with a beautiful woman."

"Thank you."

"Can I talk to you a minute?" Alyssa asked him.

He looked to Ayanna and then back to Alyssa.

"Sure." He turned back to Ayanna. "I'll be back in a few minutes. Would you like something else to eat or drink that I can order while I'm up?" he asked.

"I would love another white wine. Maybe another order of those stuffed mushrooms."

"You got it. I'll have them brought over."

Ayanna smiled and nodded as he walked away with Alyssa's arm encircled in his.

When they were in an area where they could hear each other over the crowd, he turned to her.

"You lied to me," Alyssa blurted out before he could ask her what she wanted to talk to him about.

"I did? About what?"

"I asked you if you were going to talk to Everly and you promised me you would. You lied. Joey asked you too. That makes you a double liar."

Carlos swiped his hand across his jaw in frustration. His brother and sister were putting a lot of pressure on him.

"Why can't the two of you leave this alone? There is nothing she needs to say to me that will matter."

"I'm not saying it will matter. I'm saying I think you need to hear it. A lot will come out in her trial. Don't let that be the first time you hear some of what she would reveal to you. Do you really think I don't know that you're hurting all over again? I see it."

That was it. He'd had enough of everyone telling him how he feels.

"I'm over it, sis. Seriously. Enough with you and Joey planning my life out for me. The two of you think you can read me like no other. You act as if I don't know what I want. Last I checked, I was a grown ass man who can make his own grown ass decisions. I helped her. I'm still helping her because that's just the kind of man I am. Don't read anything into that as if a story from her will change anything for me. Leave it alone. Let it go. I don't want to get loud with you. It's like you're not listening to me," he declared passionately.

"That's because I've heard from her. Don't you think I was floored when you asked us to help her? I couldn't figure out why you would do that after you knew I had some choice words about her. I put that to the side and did as you asked because I love you. I'm not saying what she has to say will fix your life. You didn't get the closure you needed when she walked away. I'm not even saying you need that anymore. I'm sorry if I'm being pushy. I only think that it's time to free you both of the past. You loved her. I've never seen you that happy and in love before."

"I may never be again."

"That's sad. I don't want that for you."

Carlos exhaled and decided to share something with her that he hadn't told anyone. He looked up, exhaled and then locked eyes with her.

"The week before the relationship ended and she rolled out with Hamilton, we were in Cabo. That trip was everything. I know we don't usually talk on a personal level, but that woman made love to me for an entire week like never before. We loved harder than I ever have with any woman in my life. Yes, the physical was amazing, but it was more than that. Just as fast as we loved, we didn't love anymore. She snatched what we had right from under me without warning. I didn't see it coming. I don't think I can ever let go of that."

"I'm not asking you to. I would never do that. I used to think that Joey was bad with the number of women in and out of his bed all the time, but you turned into someone worse. You're obsessed with doing anything to make you forget about Everly. There's only one way to do that."

"Sis, I have to go. I'm actually on a date and so are you. Your husband is waiting, I'm sure. Can you stop trying to fix my life and let me get back to doing it my way? I love you. Have a safe trip. You're doing a modeling gig while you're in California, right?"

"More like three. My agent has been trying to get me to take more gigs that have come up, but I decline them all. I don't get why people refuse to understand that I love my life raising my boys. I only agreed because Dexter is pushing me into it now that mom is going with us to look after the boys. We're staying at a house in Malibu on the beach. We've decided to turn the time into a family vacation. We'll be gone about a week and a half instead of three or four days."

"Really? Dexter is taking a vacation from work that long?"

"He needs it. So do I."

"I'm happy for you. Have fun and we'll talk when you get back. I don't want you to worry about anything that's going on here. I'll update you; I promise."

Carlos kissed her on the cheek as they walked back toward the bar.

~~

"Did you see him? Carlos is here," Everly said, speaking as if she were exhausted. What she was, was nervous.

"What? Where?" Nola asked.

"Over at the bar. He just walked in with his sister. She walked on toward the front of the room. He's standing at the end of the bar. God, he looks good."

Everly turned around in her seat at their table near the back when Nola didn't respond. What she found was a cheshire cat grin on her face that told her all she needed to know.

"You want to jump his bone, right? I mean, he's your *McDreamy*."

"Nola, it's not that cheap."

"Wait, I don't mean any disrespect. I know you love him. I wasn't making light of the situation."

Everly smiled and took Nola's hand into hers. She knew there was no harm.

"I know. You're right though. He is and I still love him. I never, ever stopped loving him. I thought about Carlos every single day that I couldn't get out from what I was under. I know he's done with me. Seeing him, I can't help it. I've never loved anyone like I did and still love him."

"Go over and talk to him. He's right there. He can't avoid you if you walk up to him."

"And say what?"

"Well, for starters, say hello."

"You make it seem so easy."

"Everly, go over there and say hi."

When Nola pushed her lightly on the shoulder, Everly stood on nervous legs. She stayed next to the table, wiping her hands down her little black dress because her palms were already sweating. This wasn't just about going over to say hello to the love of her life. This was about reclaiming her life which had been upended when she left him. He may not want her anymore, but they can't go through life as if they didn't have an amazing love affair. It was one that even now had her rubbing her legs together to relieve the desire that was building up between them at the thought of the amazing days and nights of love they shared. Carlos may not have been her first, but he had been her last; something he was under the impression wasn't true. Nola was right. They were finally in the same space. He couldn't ignore her tonight.

"Okay, I'm going in," she leaned down and whispered.

One step at a time, she thought as she moved in Carlos' direction. She made sure her dark glasses were in place and that her long blond wig covered her face as much as possible.

Making her way through people coming and going, Everly was disappointed when Carlos picked up a glass and a small plate of food handed to him by the bartender. Her eyes followed him as he walked away from the bar and over to a small table in the back of the room near the door on the opposite side of where she was sitting with Nola. Her nerves of steel from minutes ago were turned to mush the moment Carlos placed the glass in front of a beautiful woman before adding the plate to the table. Before she realized she was holding her breath, her heart sank when Carlos leaned down and kissed the woman on the lips. It wasn't just a quick peck. The kiss was long, lingering and full of, no doubt, promises of more to come. She knew what that kind of kiss felt like from him and what it could lead to. She knew the look that she could see in his eyes when he pulled away. The woman wiped lipstick from his lips before he slid into their small, romantic booth.

Feeling as if all eyes were on her because she was standing as still as a mannequin in a room full of people moving about, she began moving backwards. Afraid that Carlos may see her, she shifted to the side in a small alcove where he wouldn't be able to get a glimpse of her if he looked her way. She couldn't resist looking. He had moved on. He was seeing someone. This woman was someone special. She couldn't see Carlos' face anymore, but she could see love in the woman's eyes. Was he as in love with her as she appeared to be with him? Unable to take the brutal beating to her heart, she raced back over to her table and sat back down.

"Well? What happened? What did Carlos say?" Nola asked.

Everly waited. She had to find the words. She never imagined what she would feel if she ever saw Carlos with another woman let alone with his lips seductively on her. Finally, she could find her breath.

"He didn't say anything. He was too busy tonguing down a beautiful woman in a booth in the back. Can we leave? Please get me out of here."

So that Nola and no one else could see her crying, she rushed toward an exit that was far away from where Carlos sat. She was close to tossing back up the garlic parmesan wings and fried broccoli bites she ate. She was that sick of seeing the love of her life with someone else. This gut punch had to be what Carlos felt when she left him and ran off with Hamilton. She was getting a dose of her own medicine and she hated it. The idea of Carlos with another woman was tearing her up inside. Her last thought before they rushed off down the hall was that she got exactly what she deserved.

8

Carlos walked into his office at the casino to get his usual morning update before heading out onto the casino floor. Each day, before he did anything else, he took a stroll through every area of the casino. His team would give him the good and bad news of the evening before on a night when he was otherwise engaged.

For most of the day before, he was with Horace on the grounds of where his and Torrence's newest casino was being built. He'd left the casino security in the hands of several senior members of his staff who often stood in for him because he wore many hats.

Before he could sit down to look at several notes on his desk from his assistant, there was a knock on his office door.

"You're here already?" he asked Melvin who entered and closed the door behind him.

"I wanted to talk to you before you hit the casino floor. Are you here all day today?" Melvin asked.

"Today is my day for being here. Besides, I have several meetings set up. Joey and I are also doing a few interviews though I don't have to do those if I'm needed elsewhere. What's the latest?"

"The guys from overnight are on their way here. I was hoping to catch you first. It's about Everly."

Carlos snapped to attention the minute he heard her name.

"Oh? Something wrong?"

"Have you seen her lately?"

Carlos was nonchalant about his stance. Everyone close to him knew what was going on with him when it came to her. To even ask him that question was a joke when he knew Melvin knew the answer. He humored him.

"No, I haven't. I understand that she had a friend visit last week."

"She saw you."

Carlos looked over at him.

"What? Who saw me?"

"Everly. She saw you that night; the same night her friend was here."

"What do you mean she saw me? Stop speaking cryptic and tell me what the hell you're being all mysterious about."

"Manny was watching her from a distance to be sure no one came up to her. You said we needed to have someone looking out for her while she's here. He saw you when you were talking to your sister. You then went to the bar. Following that, back to your table."

"Everyone is supposed to watch out for her, not watch me and what I'm doing. Do I need to issue better instructions?"

Melvin held his hands up in surrender.

"Hey, I'm only the messenger. No one is following you. It just so happens that the two of you were at the concert that night."

"Everly was there? I didn't see her."

"True. She saw you. Whatever she saw had her rattled. She hustled back to her room as if she were about to breakdown."

"I'm hearing about this why?"

"Who was the woman you were lip-locked with? Do I know her? Whoever she was and whatever Everly saw, Manny said she was crying by the time she got back to her room."

His date. Everly saw him? He didn't care. They weren't involved anymore.

"Why are we having this discussion at the butt-crack of dawn?"

"That was a distraction for the real conversation I need to have with you."

"Melvin, if you don't stop whatever this is and get to the damn point!"

Carlos felt himself losing his patience with the unnecessary need Melvin often had for dragging out a conversation.

"Cecily. Her friend from New York?"

"Yeah, what about her? I asked you all to check into both of her friends as well as what the latest was with her brother."

"Nola is the one who was with her, so she's good. Cecily's sister reached out to Everly's lawyer in the middle of the night. She said she didn't have a number for Everly. She saw information about Nadine in all of the news reports about the firm representing Everly. That's how she was able to get contact information for the attorney. Nadine called me on my cell this morning. Someone attacked Cecily. She was brutally beaten inside of her own New York apartment."

Carlos' eyes widened in shock.

"What? Are you serious?"

"I'm dead-ass serious. I'm telling you this because her sister said of the few words the police and doctors were able to get from her, Cecily said two men did this to her. They were trying to get her to help them get close to Everly. They know she's here in Chicago, but don't know where. For some reason, they started with Cecily."

"Dammit. Everly did arrive in New York before coming to Chicago. This is all connected, most likely to Hamilton," Carlos noted.

"We think the only reason they didn't come for Nola is because her husband is ex-military and not as easy to get to as Cecily was. Someone is out to get your girl."

"She's not my girl. Any idea who? I'm assuming it's either Hamilton or her father. Could be a combination of them both. Either way, the situation is extremely dangerous."

"Not a clue. Everly doesn't know yet. Nadine said she hasn't told her. She wanted to know how she should handle it? Should she tell her? Should we tell her? Nadine asked if we're still planning to give more protection to her client? She can't but she hopes you or we can."

Carlos was silent. He turned his chair around so that his back was to Melvin. He needed a moment to think. He snapped his finger when he realized what was happening.

"Let's add more to Everly's detail. The news. He knows that she's been talking. He's looking for her to probably shut her up. No one knows as much about what has been going on as she does; she and her brother. He's already in jail. I doubt if he's talking. Everly is different."

"Hamilton?" Melvin questioned.

"Hamilton. He's trying to find her."

"But Cecily was in New York. Why not start in Chicago?"

"Because everyone Everly knows is in Chicago. He wouldn't dare. Like you said, if they tried for Nola, they would have encountered her mountain of a husband. No one goes up against him or comes for his family; not if they like living. You only need to google his name to know all you need to about staying far away from him and what belongs to him."

"Man, they beat that woman bad," Melvin explained.

"He's also thinking that if Everly is here, she came to me for help."

"What exactly are you saying? Are you thinking Hamilton is back in this country?"

"I don't know. He definitely has contacts. Maybe not contacts on that level, but someone does. There are more people than Hamilton involved in the scheme. There's no telling who could have done this. With Everly's testimony, she will bring down a lot of powerful men. I don't know the entire story of who's involved hasn't gotten out. People are being protected. The only target appears to be Everly."

"I can make sure she's protected, but we need to know who we are up against. Are you okay if I talk to her? I need to know who we're looking out for. You good with that?"

Carlos waited. Then he knew.

"No, I'm not. I have a different play in mind. There is a lot to unpack here. I need to know that we're going about this the right way. Again, no, I'm not."

"No? I wasn't expecting that. I thought you wanted me to make sure no one got near her. I need to know who these people are. We need to know how ruthless they are."

"I think you know that if her best friend was attacked it's because someone is out for her. I didn't say no because I don't want you to get the information. I said it because I'm going to talk to her and get what you need. How is Cecily doing?"

"I was checking with you on getting someone to check to find out."

Carlos was thinking of a better master plan. It wasn't just Everly who needed protection. He would reach out to Nola's husband as soon as his conversation with Melvin ended. They were friends. He would warn him to be on the lookout for danger that may come his way. He pitied anyone who would try. First, he needed to do what he could for Cecily.

"Who do we have on the east coast providing security to someone? I think we have two guys with Pedro, that Miami based singer. Two guys with the R&B singer, Allysin. Anybody else?"

"Two veterans and one new guy on the Baltimore Ravens quarterback. What are you thinking?"

"Cecily. Connect with them. Send two new guys from here to assist. I would feel better if you could make the trip there and scope out what's going on. Perhaps get Cecily and her sister someplace safe? Definitely have someone on Cecily in the hospital while she's there. I have a friend in the NYPD that you can reach out to. He's a detective; one of the best to ever do it. Also, check with Reese's brother, DJ. He used to work for the NYPD. He may have some folks we can trust to also help."

"I can be there in a few hours. I won't let her out of my sight."

"Take one of the new guys with you. Reach out to Nadine. Have her put you in touch with Cecily's family. I don't care how much protection the NYPD think they'll be doing, they have no clue. Let's use all of the resources we have."

"What about Everly? She has another deposition tomorrow afternoon. I can shift a few guys around to be sure we have the best on her. The media are like hawks out looking for their prey. They are trying to find her."

"I get that. Get Deidre on her in your absence."

Melvin made note on his phone for what he needed to do next.

"No more concerts or other public events for her that I don't know about. She may not get how serious this whole case is. There are a lot of people who would love to see her dead. That had better not happen on my watch or I will burn Chicago to the ground. You handle New York. I've got Everly. I'll go speak with her this week. I have a busy couple of days, but then I'll carve out the time to talk to her in depth. I know she's going to hate this, but she shouldn't leave her suite unless it's about the case."

"I know why you may not have seen her last night."

"Oh?"

"Manny said she was in a long blond wig and some fancy glasses. I won't say what she had on because I already told Manny to stop looking at her so closely. She's still beautiful, bro. That's all I'm going to say."

"Off-limits. Tell that to Manny. Whatever he's thinking, he had better bury it. Do I need to explain to him why?"

Carlos saw the smile that graced Melvin's face when he cocked an eye his way.

"She's yours. You don't have to say it. Never admit it if you don't want to. I get it. We've been friends a long time. Don't play me. I know what she meant and still means to you. I was there the night she showed up here. You were practically hysterical in a cool, calm and collected kind of way. I know you. She was in trouble and you were relieved that she came here to you. I'm on the next flight out. I'll take Jimmy with me. He's new and could learn a thing or two about surveillance and security. I'll check in with you later tonight. You've got

Everly? You're sure? We have a lot of people we can put on her tomorrow."

"The team stays the same except that I'll be replacing you as point as long as Everly doesn't have a problem with that. I don't want her feeling uncomfortable. That could lead to mistakes. I'm not free tomorrow. Deidre will do great. After that, I'll make the time."

"Mistakes with you in charge? Hell no. I can't even imagine that. No one would protect her better than you. I hope the conversation about her friend goes well. You need to do that soon. I'm sure the story will hit the news. It may reach Chicago sooner rather than later."

"I got it covered. Why don't you let the team from last night in so that they can go home and get some sleep before returning tonight. I understand we had no issues last night at all."

"Other than a few people who had too much to drink and made fools of themselves, it wasn't a bad night. We were crowded to the max. How are the plans going with the new casino?"

"No major issues."

"I understand Horace is here from Vegas. Is he here for a while?"

"He is here. We're all hanging out this weekend. It's been a while since Carter, Torrence, DJ, Tucker, Joey and I have hung out. We're going to miss Dexter who is still in Los Angeles with my sister and the kids. Horace is here for a while, maybe even permanently. Besides, he's going to be running this place as well. Torrence is going to step back now that his wife is pregnant. He wants to step back some to focus on Reese. Horace is cool. He's good people. I want him to personally meet every guy we're putting on that site," Carlos explained.

"Sounds like a plan. Before I leave, let me know what else you need. Make sure you watch your own back. The way Nadine described how Everly's friend was beaten, they aren't playing. Whoever this is, Everly is in a lot of danger."

Carlos knew that to be true. He's been doing some research on Arlo Campos and he comes from that true Chicago mob scene. Some people may think that life was over and done with but it's not. It's just a little more underground which is where Arlo is as well.

"I appreciate the warning. I'm always ready for whatever. I would never let anyone come into my city and hurt my...uh, hurt Everly. Like I said, not on my watch."

Carlos shook his head from side to side when he realized the slip of the tongue he'd just made. Melvin, no doubt, caught it too by the look on his face.

"I hear you. Also, I heard you. You won't let anyone hurt your woman. She still is, you know. The sad part of all of this is that you're the only person who hasn't really grasped that she is yours. I don't care what happened, you are still in love with Everly. I'll leave it at that. I'll send the team in to debrief and then I'm out."

For the few minutes he would be left alone before his office was flooded with six members of his team who oversaw the entire casino security force from the night before. Carlos thought about that Freudian slip of the tongue. Melvin was right. Despite all that Everly had taken him through and done to him, he still saw her as his. He was stupid for that, yes. Thinking like that is how he was so vulnerable to be hurt by her before. This time, being around her, he would know to be on guard against everything he thought he knew and loved about her. Her story was as old as time. She played him. Now she was here asking for his help. He would provide it but that was the extent of their involvement.

His office door opened and he waved everyone in. They would have their meeting and then he needed to go handle some business while he thought of how he would approach Everly about what happened to Cecily. She was going to be crushed especially if she finds that the attack was because of her. It's possible, someone Hamilton or her father had in place had watched her while she was in New York. Now that he knew how potentially dangerous this was all getting, he would be ready for anything. He needed to keep Everly close. How close will depend on their first real interaction since she arrived in Chicago. He was ready. He hoped she was ready for him. Besides, he felt the need to explain what she may have seen when he was out with Alyanna. He didn't owe Everly an explanation but he wasn't dirty. He still didn't want to see her hurt, especially by him.

9

Why Cecily wasn't answering her call or calling her back was starting to get to Everly. She and Nola were two people that she had come to depend on since she returned. She and Nola had established a pattern of when to contact each other. Cecily had gone on-contact. There were no messages, texts or calls of any kind. Nola said even she had not heard from Cecily in a few weeks. They had even jumped on a three-way call the night before and still, no Cecily. As a traveling author, it wasn't out of the ordinary for Cecily to be out of commission when her schedule got crazy. Everly remembered checking Cecily's travel schedule on her website and saw that she should have been at home in New York for the next few weeks. Perhaps, the real truth was that Cecily had heard of the story around her life and decided she didn't want any parts of it. After all, when she left with Hamilton, she pretty much gave everyone in her life the middle finger, including Cecily. This may be her payback.

Her desperation to reach her friend was now turning to worry. They have had good and bad days as friends over the years. Not one of those bad times did either of them just ignore the other.

As she paced around the bedroom in her suite still bored out of her mind having to stay inside all the time, she was about to call Cecily again when her phone rang. The number was unfamiliar, but was a Chicago exchange. Hesitantly, she answered with more of a question that a statement.

"Hello?"

"Everly."

That voice. Just hearing it her body tingled. His voice, his very presence did that to her. He was calling her. She didn't know what to say or how to act. Her head was doing a happy dance. This was a call to her phone and not to her room. The image of him kissing that woman a few days ago still lived rent free in her head. She didn't let that ruin her happiness at hearing his voice on the other end.

"Carlos. Um, hi."

"Surprised?" he asked.

She smiled and sat on the navy-blue seat at the foot of her bed. Her legs trembled as his handsome face splayed across her mind. She had no right to him or to images of him that thrilled every sexy orifice of her body.

"I am. You've only called my room once and never my new cell. I didn't know you still had the number."

"I've had it since you got it. For some reason, my meddling sister thought that I should have it."

"Meddling? Do you know that if she hadn't meddled, I would be in this city all alone? She and your friends have been a lifeline thanks to you. If I haven't said thank you enough, I'm saying it again."

"Don't. I get it and you're welcome. How are you? How are things going? Were you busy?"

"Oh, no, I'm not busy. Just in this room as usual. Your team and my attorney are seeing to that. I hear it dangerous out in these streets for me. It's a quiet existence, that's for sure."

"You get why, right?"

"I do. These walls are closing in on most days, but yes, I get it. I'll take this over a jail cell."

Everly grimaced at the thought of where she could be compared to the room she was in. She would not continue to complain.

"Very true. Your current view is a much better option. Hopefully, your attorney can make a view outside of jail permanent. I meant to call before today to ask how you were doing after the altercation outside of the courthouse. I get that's been a few short weeks ago. You know how busy work can get for me."

"Carlos, it's okay; I promise. I was rattled for a few days. People want my head on a platter though I didn't steal their money; Hamilton and his cronies did. That includes my father. I know I'm tied to it. I'm left to deal with it. Thanks for getting me out of there. Nadine said that it was you who came up with the plan that got me back to the hotel safely. You keep saving me. I don't want to be a burden."

Even after the words left her mouth, she knew Carlos would make it clear that she wasn't, no matter their past.

"No worries. You're not a burden. I want you to be safe."

"Things could have been really bad that day. Thank goodness I only hurt my leg. It's still a little sore from where I fell against the car. I was hoping to go workout in the gym."

"I know how much you love working out, but you can't. Not in a public gym. Your face is recognizable at this point. Any photos of you could have the press living outside of the hotel."

"I know. I may at least order a machine for in my room, perhaps a cycle or something. Nadine was able to get my trust fund unlocked after everything I have was seized. That can't be touched since it was put aside for me as a child. I'm not going to go overboard with spending it. Something to work out on would help take the edge off."

Workout. Everly's thoughts turned from the gym and to their idea of working out back when they were a couple. She loved that it involved going outside of the lines of intimacy. It's borderline wild magnetism that had them bursting at the seams with untamed lust. As soon as the thought came to the surface, she then imagined Carlos with the woman she saw him with and what they would have done together. It's only natural that she would be jealous; and she was.

"If you like, I can recommend something that you would like. I ordered one as a gift for my sister after she had her second baby. She didn't like being away from the boys to go to the gym. She now has a full gym at home."

"Yes. I trust you. I would appreciate that."

"Good. Consider that done. I'll send you a link to your phone. Or, I can show you on mine. I'm hoping you'll be okay if I come by to talk. I have a meeting with my team who are about to travel with Joey and Marlow for his next wrestling match. His popularity is crazy. I can stop by when I'm done if that works."

"I've been in this room so much that the walls are closing in. Can we go someplace other than my room to talk? Is there a quiet room or space in the casino? I'll take anything that's not here. I can even wear one of the disguises I use when I go out for court."

When there was a long pause, Everly assumed he was going to go against that idea. She thought that he would remind her of how unsafe that could be. She waited.

"How about my suite? We can talk privately there," he offered.

That small option had her dancing in her head. She wasn't going to have any expectations other than being grateful that he was understanding her desire for a little more space. As much as they like going out and traveling, Carlos had to know that she was going stir-crazy.

"You don't mind?"

"Not at all. I'll swing by to pick you up once I'm done."

"Thanks Carlos."

"Anytime. I'll call you in a little while."

Once the call ended Everly stood and walked around in a circle. She and Carlos were going to talk. Not only that, but she would get to see where he lives and spends his time in the hotel when he's not knee deep in work. Perhaps, little by little, he would allow her back into his life if for no other reason than a friend. Being away from him made her realize that he had, in fact, been her very best friend. She hated that she ruined that by choosing wrong. This was wishful thinking, she knew.

She was excited. In fact, excitement overwhelmed her as she spun herself around and shrieked with joy. Tossing her phone into the air, it rang the second it left her hand. She grabbed it before it hit the bed and answered immediately thinking it was Carlos already calling back.

"Hello!"

"Hey Everly. It's Marlow. Just checking in on you. Joey and I are going out of town for a few days. I'm sorry I won't be able to stop by to see you before we leave."

"Carlos just mentioned that you and Joey would be out of town at a wrestling match. It's all good. I hope the match will be televised so that I can watch it."

"It should be. I'll check to be sure so that you can watch it on the right network. So, you talked to Carlos? That's intriguing."

Everly was cheesing with glee.

"I did. He called me and asked if we could talk later. He said he had a meeting but would come by."

"Progress?" Marlow asked.

"I don't know. Whatever it is, I'll take it."

"In case he mentions this after his meeting with Joey that's taking place in about an hour, my doctor informed us that all the problems I've been experiencing are because I'm pregnant!"

"Pregnant? You and Joey? Wow! That is so exciting. Congratulations to you. You've been under the weather for a little minute. Pretty much since the night I came back. Unless you were feeling out of sorts before then."

"That night was the trigger to me not feeling like myself and realizing it. I had been so busy that my mind was on other things. I never suspected. Life has been so crazy that being pregnant was the furthest from my mind. Joey is as excited as I am. That's why I'm going with him on this trip. He wasn't going to go if I didn't go with him. He's protective of me and now of me and the baby. He worries considering how horrible I've been feeling."

"Girl, go with your man and have fun. I admire you. I've always wanted a bunch of children. Carlos and I used to talk about that back when we were together. Old dreams I guess," she lamented.

So much about her life was on a path she didn't want to be on. She and Carlos would have been amazing parents; something she never had after her mother was gone. She now knows that her mother had been killed and didn't walk away from her and Dante. She had questioned if she would make a great mother after not having much success at learning from the example of her parents.

"You still have time."

Everly nodded and wondered how true those words were. She only wanted to have Carlos' babies; no one else's. She was far from that.

"I sure hope so," she said with her thoughts on a life of babies with Carlos on her mind.

"When all of this court business is done, maybe you could come over to the house. Joey said it used to be your house. Wait until you see the changes he's made to the place. I love our house."

"I'll look forward to that if I'm a free woman after all of this."

"I'm claiming freedom for you. I believe there is something greater for you at the end of this. Don't be too down about your current situation. I was at a low point in my life when I met Joey. I was down on life and about to move away from the city I love just to get a fresh start. I didn't think that was possible here due to family issues. Hitting Joey's car was horrible, but it put me on this current path of a love beyond anything I could have ever dreamed of. Now, if I could just find my sister. That would be the icing on the cake for me."

"No luck yet? Any more mysterious phone calls?"

"Not recently. Carlos has a person on his team working with a private investigator that he works with who is looking for Angel. He's searching in the Florida area, but I get a feeling that Angel is closer. I think she may be in the Chicago area. I'm never going to give up on having her back home. I was about to give up on everything. I'll never do that again. There is always hope. I say the same about you and Carlos. Joey told me a lot about the two of you and how things went down. I know from talking to you that you are still madly in love with him. Even though I crashed into Joey and could have ruined his life and his career, he loves me unconditionally. That kind of love may sometimes take a detour but it doesn't go away all together. If there is a way for the two of you to connect, it will happen. I want you to have faith. Have it in your court case and have it when it comes to Carlos. Joey has forgiven you. Alyssa has also forgiven you. Maybe once you and Carlos talk, he will forgive you too."

Keeping hope alive, Everly half-smiled. She wasn't as sure about that as Marlow was.

"I'm going to take the opportunity to tell him everything tonight. He may not totally forgive me. I am praying for understanding if nothing else."

"I'm routing for you and for Carlos. You could both use a win. He's a great guy."

"He's the best guy; the only guy as far as I'm concerned."

"Fight for him, Everly. Until there is nothing left to fight for, fight for him."

"Thanks for the encouragement. Even if he only lets me get out what I want to say, that's enough for me. He has to know the truth. I'm the only person who can tell it to him."

"Good luck. I'm going to get dinner ready for when Joey finishes with his meeting. I'll talk to you when I get back. Good luck for your next deposition. Give Hamilton hell by telling all the lies he's been selling people for a long time. You got this!" Marlow said.

Everly was encouraged as she pumped her fist in the air like a champion.

Tossing her phone to the bed, she went to her closet to look for the perfect outfit to wear. Carlos may hate her for what she did to him but that won't keep her from showing him what he's missing out on.

Being honest with herself, she came back to Chicago for him. She came back to reclaim the love that lies and deceit took from her due to her own need to protect those around her. She'd lost him. If she could get him back, she was going for it starting tonight.

10

Carlos didn't expect that being around Everly for more than a few minutes would be this torturous. It was hell but in a good way. The moment she opened her door to him and his eyes landed on her, he was a goner. He was all set to continue with his hard, unbothered exterior. That failed the minute he saw her. Her beautiful smile melted the ice he'd held around his heart since she returned to Chicago. She was still so amazingly beautiful.

Without realizing he was doing so, his eyes took in every gorgeous one of her curves. He was suddenly reminded that it never mattered how many women he bedded, and there had been a lot over the past year, he was never going to wipe from his mind how good he and Everly were when it came to sex. It had always been astonishingly mind-blowing and downright soul-stirring. That's where his mind went when she opened the door. Her clothes fell away and his head had him picking her up and finding a spot to bury himself deep without her pillowy walls, not just massaging his body but his very soul. He was also questioning why he never had that feeling with other women. He got in them and out, receiving the immediate release he wanted. After, he felt empty because there was no connection. His true connection was standing in front of him. Everly was the reason no other woman did it for him like her. She, of all people, had to be that one. He hated that, while at the same time, regaled at the after effect of being with her.

Everly stood before him in a sexy white sleeveless top that enhanced the sexiest cleavage he'd ever seen and he's seen a lot of them. She had on a cute knee-length navy skirt with heels that matched. Legs. Everly had legs for days. When he discovered he stood before her with no words being exchanged, he cleared his throat in hopes that it would clear his mind. No such luck. Did he imagine she greeted him? He was too focused on the image before him and not the words coming out of her mouth; and what a sexy mouth she had. It was covered in a glossy sheen. Did he just image her licking her lips, slow and methodically or was he hallucinating? Either way, he was being charmed like a moth to a flame. It was clear, he had little will-power when it came to her. He mentally shook off the new state of arousal and rejoined the moment in order to save face. He wanted to reach down to adjust the movement behind his zipper but that would be too obvious. No way did he want her eyes to travel to that part of him that he clearly had little to no control over.

"You look beautiful. Are you ready to go?" he asked when he could find his tongue again. For a few seconds, it was lusting after Everly.

"Thank you. Yes, I'm ready. I need to grab my wallet and phone just in case you've decided that we can be adventurous and I can get out of this hotel," she joked.

"Not on your life. I could swing it, but maybe on a night when I'm not exhausted."

"You're beat, huh?" she asked.

"I am, but it's all good. Besides, it's still daylight. You would be recognized."

"I knew I should have put on a wig," she kidded further.

"Another time. Besides, I've always loved your hair all natural."

Carlos let go of the yawn he'd been holding in. He'd been up, pretty much around the clock, for the past few days running from one job or meeting to the next. As busy as he was, he was looking forward to a night of downtime; something he rarely got or took advantage of.

"Are you sure you're up for talking tonight? I know you're a busy man. That yawn looked like it covered days of no sleep."

"Not too busy for you. I'm a little tired, but I'm good to talk tonight. I'm going to order dinner for us when we get to my suite. We can both relax and talk."

Carlos stood at the door while Everly rushed to get what she needed and then joined him.

"What floor are you on?" she asked.

"Sixteenth floor," he explained as they walked.

"Wow! I bet that view is beautiful."

"Well, when we get there, let me know what you think. I like the view. I don't get to enjoy it as much as I would like to. I'm either on the job here, onsite at a location or at my office downtown."

"You have an office outside of the casino?"

"I do. I run my private security company in a separate building. It's a good thing because Joey and I are about to expand and will need the space that the building will give us. In fact, it's in the same building where Reese has her marketing firm. There was empty office on the entire second floor and before someone snatched it up, she told me about it knowing I was on the lookout for something reasonably priced. The floor below us is up for grabs after a law firm on that level moved out into a smaller space. I was at a meeting with Joey earlier to secure that floor as well. We're growing fast and sweet."

When they reached the elevator, he stepped to one side once inside. Something told him to keep his distance until the desire to hold her wore off. He expected to have some feelings about her resurface, but not as strong as they had. He was a man in trouble. He was a man still in lust and in love. That much was obvious as they rode in silence to his floor.

They walked in silence until he opened the door to his suite and allowed her to go in before him. Once inside, he closed the door and leaned back against it as the room lit up with lights once they stepped in far enough for the automatic light sensors to kick in. Everly moved ahead of him and looked around.

"I'm sorry, can I?" she asked him before looking further.

"Sure, go ahead. Make sure you go over to the window to check out the view. It's especially nice at night. With the sun going down, you can get an early look of how beautiful it will get when it's completely dark out there. You can see lights for miles."

Everly did just that. He could see the excitement all over her.

"I thought I was seeing something on the seventh floor. I would sleep right here on this window ledge."

"It's definitely perfect."

Carlos said the words but wasn't talking about the view outside. He was speaking of the view of Everly inside of his suite.

"I remember seeing the framework of this casino before..."

When she stopped, he knew why. He and Torrence weren't friends at the time, but the construction started back even before he and Everly were a couple. They had talked a few times about how much fun they would have visiting the casino once it opened. That was when they were a couple. A lot changed for them in a short period of time.

"It's okay," he said moving away from the door. "I know what you started to say. Anyway, this is home until I figure out what I want outside of here. I'm thinking about a condo because of the low maintenance. In that way, I am completely different than my brother. He loves his house. Backyard grilling and gatherings are his thing. Speaking of, I was with him before I came to get you and he told me that he and Marlow are having a baby. That is some incredible news. Did Marlow tell you how they met?"

"That's wonderful news. She shared that with me when I talked to her earlier. She did tell me the story of their meeting. It was literally by accident; the actual crash kind of accident. Her story taught me that no matter the start, or the stuff in between, it's how you end up. They are living their happily ever after. Do you think you'll stay in Chicago permanently once your company expands beyond Chicago? It has to. You're good at what you do. I saw an article about you and your security agency on the plane ride from South American to New York. You're at the top of the list for one of the most successful bachelors to watch in the coming year. That's a great achievement. You must be pleased with how you've sprouted and grown."

"I think I've found where I want to be. All of my family is here. I did love Vegas. Joey and I were there for a while. Chicago has grown on me. I have amazing friends. My businesses are here. I'm also under contract to provide the security for the new casino Torrence and his partner, Horace are building. All of my family is finally in the same place. I don't want to shake that up. I'm working on being happy here."

"Business is booming for you. I'm happy for all that's coming your way. You deserve it. I believe you can be happy wherever you are. You're right that family matters. I didn't have much of that. Seeing yours so close, I get it."

Carlos wanted to change the subject. At one point, he imagined them as happy as Alyssa and Dex and Marlow and Joey. He was first to fall in love. Now he was pulling up the rear as the last person standing up against a permanent type of relationship. He wasn't sure he was meant to have that after all.

"Can I get you something to drink? I need to order dinner. Do you know what you'd like?"

"I don't. I am hungry. I'm thinking something Italian. Do you have any wine? White or red would work. If not, water is fine too."

"You're in luck. One of the best Italian restaurants in Chicago is right here in the casino. I have red and white wine. I'll get the red."

Carlos went in search of the tablet so that they could look at the menu options for the night. After handing her the tablet, he went into the kitchen to find the wine. He needed to remember the main reason for wanting to talk to her. It was clear that so far, she hadn't heard about what happened to

Cecily. He needed to tell her. It was going to be hard. Still, it had to be done. That meant that her friend, Nola wasn't aware either. If Everly had been keeping up on news out of New York, she would know. He'd been made aware earlier that the story had made the news and reports of the attack were spreading wide. Today had to be the day.

With wine and glasses in hand, he invited her to join him at the small dining set so that they could talk. He poured them each a glass.

"You're so serious. Is everything okay? I know you wanted to talk but you never said what it was about. I'm hoping to talk to you too, if you will allow me to go back and explain things."

Carlos nodded. He assumed that they would eventually talk about what was the elephant between them. When he asked her to get together to talk, he knew their past would come up. He had prepared himself to hear what she had to say. He'd dodged that talk long enough.

"For a while, I didn't want you to explain things to me. I've tried to stay on the outside of everything. I didn't think I needed to relive any part of our past in order to get people in place to help you," he admitted.

"You've changed your mind?"

Carlos took a moment to consider how the news would hit her. He decided to approach it like ripping off a bandage.

"Recent circumstances have changed my mind," he said.
"Oh?"

He inhaled deeply and put the purpose in the atmosphere.
"Cecily," he finally said.

He couldn't get out more just yet. Taking the time to gather his thoughts on how to approach the subject was key. Everly took a sip of her wine. He watched her enjoy that first taste, which was always the best. He gave her that before hitting her with the bad news.

"You know, it's weird that you would mention her. I have been trying to call her for the past few days pretty much nonstop. I'm getting nothing by way of response from her. That's not like her at all. I mean, there has been no contact at all from her. Even times when I've pissed her off, she has always responded. She has to know what's going on. I want her to hear what's really going on from me."

"Like I said, I haven't wanted to know about the entire situation myself. Now, I need to know. This conversation is going to start with Cecily," he explained.

"Cecily? Why her? Wait, what's going on? What do you know?"

His face had to be his tell. She had to be able to read him. Everly always could. What he also remembered was how emotional she could get when it came to bad news. She never had a sister so her sisterly bond with Cecily and Nola was strong. They were both a strong presence during the time that they were together. He needed to get over the peak in order to let her get through the immediate shock of what happened.

"Everly, your friend was attacked in her apartment in New York. It's pretty bad, but she's okay. I sent Melvin there to provide protection until we get more information on what happened. According to Cecily's sister, who reached out to Nadine because this involves you, the men who attacked her and beat her pretty bad were looking for information about you. They wanted to know where you were. It seems they were able to track your movements to her place."

"Wait - what! Cecily is hurt? Looking for me? Is she going to be okay? Oh, my god. She was attacked by men looking for me? Hamilton's men? Men sent from my dad? Who? Oh, my god! I can't believe it."

When her voice cracked, Carlos knew what was next. He was worried when she turned as pale as a ghost right before his very eyes. Her light skin was turning white, almost ashen. When she abruptly stood and placed her hand over her heart, he stood with her. He didn't reach for her but wanted to make sure he was close if she needed someone to physically lean on. What scared him the most was that she wasn't speaking. She had a look on her face like she wanted to say something but the words wouldn't come out. He kept quiet while she took in the few words that he'd said. They played in his mind again. Cecily had been attacked because of Everly. That had to be hard for her to hear. It had been painful for him to say.

"I think she's going to be okay. Melvin will check in with me in a few hours. I know he's landed a few days ago and made his way to the hospital. The last I heard from him was that NYPD has a man stationed outside of her hospital room around the clock. Melvin also has a guy close by on watch. Cecily is well protected and will be until she doesn't need it anymore."

"You mean while Hamilton and my dad are on the loose. I get it. The attack was them. It had to be. I've pissed off a lot of people, but they're here in Chicago. They wouldn't know about my friendship with Cecily. Hamilton would. What have I done!" she yelled.

Everly placed her hands at her temples and rubbed them. Carlos' eyes followed her as she paced around in a small circle saying she was sorry over and over.

He wanted to explain more but the look on Everly's face told him she couldn't take anymore. When she turned even paler, he moved toward her. She backed away as tears streamed down her face. It was evident she was beating herself up inside. He didn't want that.

"I'm going to be sick," she was able to stutter out.

Grabbing her hand, he rushed her into the bathroom. The moment she placed her hand over her mouth. He knew what was next. They'd made it just in time because she heaved and planted her face into the toilet. Reacting quickly, he reached for her hair and held it back while at the same time rubbing her back to console her. The idea that Cecily was hurt because of her had to cut her deep. He waited out the torrents that racked Everly's body. He remained silent and allowed her to have the reaction she needed to have. When he felt like she was done, he reached for a washcloth that was hanging on a rack near the sink. He quickly wet it and placed it on her forehead. She let it sit there for a few minutes before taking it to wipe her mouth. He helped her stand.

"I'm so sorry for that," she cried softly. "Why? Why would anyone do that to her? I need to go see her."

"Everly, you can't leave Chicago. If you do, your bail will be revoked. I promise you that as soon as I get an update from Melvin, I'll get you in contact with her sister. She can keep you updated. The contact has to be through me. We can't risk anyone discovering that the two of you are in contact. Melvin will handle that on his end and I'll handle it here. Trust me. Let me take care of this. Come sit down."

Everly nodded and walked with him to the sectional in his living room. Once she was seated, he leaned her back and placed the washcloth against her forehead. Her head shot right back up and the washcloth fell to her lap.

"Nola! What about Nola? She was here to visit me a few days ago. You have to check on her. Is she okay? Can we call and find out."

"Nola is fine. You know who her husband is. No one will ever come for her. To be on the safe side, I reached out to him the minute I heard about Cecily. He's been watching out. He is telling Nola tonight. I'm sure you'll be hearing from her soon. Trust me, she is okay."

Everly nodded and laid her head back. Carlos reached, grabbed the washcloth and placed it back on her forehead.

"I've hurt so many people," she uttered slowly.

"Everly..."

"Don't. I know you. You're going to say something like, it wasn't my fault because I allowed Hamilton to manipulate me. I was a victim. I didn't physically hurt Cecily. I get it. The truth is, I am at fault for all of this."

Carlos came around and sat next to her. He turned to her when she sat up and looked in his direction. Before his next words, he stared. There had been so many days and nights when he'd looked in her eyes like he was doing now and found the love and comfort he prayed he had also freely given her when she wanted and needed it. For the life of him, he couldn't understand why she would betray him for Hamilton. Instead of coming up with his own ideas of what happened, this was his chance to hear from Everly herself. Now was the time. He was ready to brace his ears to accept what he would hear without judging or getting angrier than he had been on the day that she'd left him.

"Talk to me. Tell me what you want me to know," he finally said.

"I want you to know all of it."

Everly's attention darted from him to her hands which she wringed again and again in her lap. He remembered her tell-tale sign of being nervous. Carlos reached over and moved her head so that her attention was back on him. If they were going to finally talk, he needed to see her eyes as she spoke.

"I'm listening," he said.

Good or bad, he would be open to it all.

Everly took in a deep breath and then let it out. His eyes went to her chest, a place he loved to lay his head. He never forgot that she has the most amazing breasts. Shaking off the thought so that his lust for her didn't distract him from her words, he raised his eyes and connected his with hers.

"I'm going to say something that I probably shouldn't say. I don't want you to react in any way. I'm not saying it to get a rise out of you in any way. I just need to get this out."

His body stirred the moment she said the word rise. He was still a goner for her beauty. His eyes focused on her lips and the way she used to cover his entire body with kisses. He coughed to again shake off his salacious thoughts with every word she says and every part of her that he laid eyes on that still gave him the rise of his life.

"Okay. No reaction. Got it," he acknowledged. "I pink swear," he joked.

"I *love* you. I know that's crazy to hear from me after what I've done, but it's the honest truth. What I did had a lot to do with the deep love I had and still have for you."

Carlos couldn't hear that right now until he got the most important question answered first.

"Hamilton?" he asked and then wished he hadn't. He needed to know.

"I never loved Hamilton. I didn't even like him. He had me by the throat with threats against my brother and against you."

That he knew. One of the things that Joey had shared with him was that Hamilton had somehow threatened him in order to get Everly to do what he wanted. He had used who her father was in order to get her in line. Arlo had been known to have killed in the past. He assumed that what it took to get Everly away from hm.

"I can take care of myself. You had to know that."

"I wasn't thinking about that back then. I was too scared. Hamilton somehow, connected with my father. I still don't know the how and when, but he did. My father is as ruthless as they come. There was a lot about him that I didn't know until I ended up in South America at his home. I should call it a dark mansion. Hamilton is the vice behind what I'm being charged with. In the midst of you and I being in love, Hamilton came up with a scheme while working for his father's investment firm. I'm not sure his father knew what was happening behind his back at that time. I wondered if he was a part of it. I came to realize he wasn't. Hamilton had too much access to get away with a scheme to steal the hard-earned retirement funds of people around the world who invested in his father's firm thinking their life savings were protected; they weren't."

"You don't know how he connected to your father? That's so random."

"It's not. From what I was able to find out, Hamilton had been dipping into some of the larger accounts. One of those accounts just happened to have been money my father had invested. When he discovered the discrepancy, he reached out to the firm and was directed to Hamilton. My father is much smarter than Hamilton on his best day; I found that out first-hand as well. When he couldn't explain himself and instead of turning Hamilton in, my father asked him how he was able to get his hands on the money without being caught. He had Hamilton in a bind. In their discussions, the connection to me and my brother came up. My father's criminal mind kicked in. Though Hamilton was able to get into some accounts and lift money, including one of my father's, he wooed my father with a way to get his hands on more money. My father was all about the money. He told Hamilton secrets about my family; mainly my brother and I. It seems, he'd kept tabs on us all these years but never reached out to us. My brother was set up by Hamilton and my dad in a major drug and human trafficking sting. Hamilton approached me with either I help him and my dad or my brother would go to jail for the rest of his life. He showed me pictures of men my father had killed. I was terrified when he said that the same could happen to you. He warned me that if I told you, my father would follow through on his plan to hurt you. I was told that what they needed me for was temporary. I started helping them while we were together. When they got greedy, that's when they needed me to leave the country."

"He blackmailed you? Why didn't you come to me with this? I could have helped you. I don't fear men like Hamilton or your father."

Hearing this made him mad as hell. Hamilton had come for his woman and snatched her way from him by using her love for her brother and for him; the only other family she knew of.

"My father is an awful man. How awful I didn't discover until recently. I knew he was a very bad man. I had heard stories for a lot of years about how he was involved in murderous doings even while living here in Chicago and in other states. He moved around a lot until he was close to getting caught. That's when he left the country and stayed under the protection of men and guns. The way he was able to reach people and have their lives snuffed out was diabolical. Still, he had connections. He threatened not only my brother's life, his own son, but your life was threatened every day. They reminded me how close they could get to you. Hamilton once showed me an image of you at a wrestling match where Joey was in the ring and you were in the seats watching. In the photos, there was a man sitting right behind you with a gun. He told me that he could have had that man put a bullet in your head with one phone call. I was scared."

"No, Everly."

"Yes. I swear, none of what I did was a reflection of a lack of love for you. That wasn't the only time. There were several. I was so scared of what my father and Hamilton would do to you and my brother. The only way I could get them away from you and my brother was to play along. I had to leave you in order to protect you. It hurt me to hurt you the way I did, but I hope you can believe me when I say I didn't think I had a choice."

Carlos reached for her hand and held it tight in his. He looked in her eyes just as tears began to fall.

"You left me and went to another country with Hamilton. You made me believe that you loved him; that you'd married him. I got a copy of your marriage license sent to me in a text message from your phone telling me that I should forget about you because you were in love with Hamilton. I still have that text," he shared.

Everly's mouth opened into an "O". When she cried to the point that her body shook, Carlos did what his heart said, but his mind said not to. He pulled her into a tight embrace. He felt her hesitation before she wrapped her arms around his neck and held on. He allowed her to cry it all out. It was clear this was a moment that they needed to have.

"I'm sorry," she said softly next to his ear.

"I know you didn't marry him. I recently found out that it was all a lie. He wanted to get to me the only way he knew he would be able to."

"All of it was a lie. I've ever only loved you; wanted you," she admitted.

Without letting her go, he knew he had to know. His point was to not look in her eyes when she answered. It was a question he had to have an answer to.

"Did you and Hamilton..."

He couldn't even get the words out without seeing fire at what her answer could be. He immediately felt anxiety and worry the minute the words left his mouth.

"No!" she shouted and moved back so that they were eye to eye again. "No, no, no. I never allowed Hamilton to touch me. I never, ever touched him. You are still the last man I ever kissed and made love to. I'm sorry that you had to spend all this time wondering about that. I know it's what he and I made you believe, but it wasn't true. I'm so sorry for the hell you went through. It was the only way I knew of to make sure Hamilton believed you were completely out of my life."

"He goaded me with the idea that something had been going on with the two of you behind my back. It wasn't until I changed my number that I no longer got these mysterious texts from him."

"He had an unhealthy rivalry with you for years. I didn't know how deep his jealously of you ran until I was in South America. When I asked him about motive for ruining your idea of me, he said it was jealously. He admitted that to me. He saw you and your life as perfect. He may have had money, but he never garnered the kind of attention from others that you got. He wanted to be you so bad. He actually hates you. He feigned a friendship just to get an insight into your life."

"I have to admit that I've always known that."

"He and my father used me to get legal documents they needed to get the money. I was a fresh out of law school attorney, still wet behind the ears. I stole documents from the law firm where I worked to provide my father with what he and Hamilton needed. This rabbit hole runs deep. In the end, my name is all over this, along with Hamilton's. The difference is, he's not in this country to stand trial along with me. I don't claim innocence. But I'm certainly not the instigator they think I am."

"Fast forward for me to how you arrived back in this country. Why would you come back knowing the heat was on you?"

"I loved you. I wanted to get back to you even though I knew that you wouldn't want me again. I had to get away from them. I found out that it was my father who killed my mother, leaving me and my brother as orphans. If it hadn't been for that, my brother and I wouldn't have been abused in the system. Financially, we gained from the law suit against Chicago that was filed on our behalf. You already know that the largest part of the trust fund came from money that my mother had gotten from my father. That may be the reason he killed her. I suspect the money was stolen. We were left with no family. That money put in a trust for us didn't wipe away the damage done to he and I both by two men who represented the state while abusing several children in their care. You know all about that because I shared my truth with you. I felt like I didn't have anyone. I've been used all my life by men."

Carlos' heart ached for her. He knew how alone she'd felt. He could imagine that being a point of someone getting close enough to use her. She'd always searched for love. That was something he thought that she had found with him.

"Not me. I have never used or abused you. I loved you. I wanted the world for you."

"I know. I threw it all away because I was afraid for me; for my brother; for you and your family. I need you to answer a question for me," Everly said.

Carlos waited. He was still trying to process it all.

"I'm listening."

"Do you believe me when I say I never let Hamilton touch me? I swear to you that I would never do that. I would rather die first than to let that slime touch me in any way. It was all a façade. None of it was factual. I had to say those things in order for him and my father to not come after you. I loved you then; I love you still."

He, no doubt, believed her. Though at one time after she left, he believed all that he thought was true. He believed what she said was true. Looking at her now, he knew she was finally telling her truth to him. He believed her.

"I believe you. For a long time, all I could see was you in his arms and in his bed. That ate me up inside."

"I'm so sorry."

"It's okay. I understand."

"It's not okay. You were my everything. We had a perfect life. I allowed myself to be drawn into a scheme when what I should have done was come to you."

Carlos held her hand tighter.

"Listen, I thought I needed to know more, but I don't. This has been a full day. If you're ready to go back to your room, I can walk you. You seem like this has taken a lot out of you. I know we haven't eaten. This has been a lot, especially with what happened to Cecily. We can do dinner another day."

"We can?" Everly asked.

Carlos saw the excitement in her eyes. It wasn't about the meal. It was about them being together. Them being in the same place without him continuing to act like she didn't exist. She did. They do. Then a solemn look covered her face. She was questioning herself.

Everly nodded with a look of sadness on her face. She stood and he reached for her hand. They remained that way for a few minutes before either moved or said a word.

"I get it. You don't want to be around me after what you know. There is more. If you knew that you may not want to help me anymore."

"It's not that at all. I'm forgiving. I'm not going to hold a grudge forever. It was what it was. Listen, if you're not ready to leave, I don't want you to think I'm throwing you out. I just thought that you would like some time to yourself to take it all in."

"Are you kidding? I'm in that room all the time. Thanks for the reprieve. This was something, though I'm dying to get out of this hotel and out under the sun or night sky without ducking and dodging people in order to stay alive."

Carlos let go of her hand and she looked around for her shoes. He had an idea.

"Do you want to still order food or would you like to go out for a bit?" he asked.

She turned sharply around to face him as he stood.

"Really? Where?"

"Do you have an issue putting on one of your disguises you use to get to court? I mean, it would be for safety reasons. I'd like to take you out for a drive."

"To the summit?"

The summit, he thought. That was a place outside of Chicago where they would go to drown out the world. They would park and either sit out on a blanket or in the car. It was a place in the mountains where, once they were at the top, they could see the entire city of Chicago in the distance. At night, the view was her favorite. The memories of the number of times they'd made love was an even bigger favorite.

"Um."

"You don't have to say no. I know what that place meant for us. I didn't mean to bring that up."

"No, it's okay. It's a beautiful place. I still love it too. I haven't been there since you left."

"It was our spot."

Carlos nodded. It was definitely there spot. They'd never told another person about that place. He had discovered it one day when he was training for a wrestling match. He loved finding secure roads to get a run in where there wouldn't be another living soul. The only access to the summit was through a property owned by an elder gentleman who he'd come to call his friend. He'd told him that anytime he wanted to come up to the summit, a place he too used to visit with his wife before she passed, he would give him the code to the security gate that allowed access to the private road.

"I hope the passcode still works. I haven't seen Mr. Wally in a long time, though I get a text or email here and there from him. Would you like to go for a drive? It's still early. It will be dark by the time we get there."

"That's the time of night when the view is at its prettiest. If you think it will work. I would like that. I would give anything to get out of here for some fresh air."

"We could take some food with us to eat in the car. I think we could both use a little breathing room. This was heavy."

"Let's go. I'm ready," Everly said. "And yes, food would be great. I'm still very much hungry."

"Truth is, so am I. While you change, I'll order the food and have it brought to the garage."

He didn't know if this was a good idea or not. He could use some breathing room and space to think. He wanted to do that with her.

Carlos coughed and smiled before turning away to turn off the lights and find his keys.

Everly laughed. He then laughed with her. They were thinking the same thing. Even after all they'd been through, her little quirky remarks still sent his mind to a sexy, dirty yet saucy place. Without either of them stating the obvious, they let the topic dissipate it the air.

"Let's go to your suite and get some proper attire for going incognito. I'm going to call Melvin to use his car. He's got a sleek jaguar with the darkest windows I know of. If it wasn't for the sticker on the back that let law enforcement know that he was once one of them, he would have tons of tickets for how fast he goes and for how dark his window tint is."

"It's illegal, huh?"

"Beyond illegal. Best of all, no one can see inside to know it's me and you. We won't stay out too long."

"I'll take any of it. Thanks for tonight. I wasn't sure how things would go."

"Things are still going. It's all good. Let's get out of here. Wait until you see this car."

Everly didn't care what the car looked like. She was feeling nostalgic and happy that he suggested it. Perhaps, like her, he didn't want the night to end yet.

11

Everly sat in the all-black Jaguar and crossed her fingers, her hands and her feet, all in hopes that the passcode that Mr. Wally had given Carlos some time ago still worked. The ride to the summit was the second-best experience of the night. The first had been to spend time with Carlos and finally being able to share with him that she had never stopped thinking about him or loving him. He didn't respond in kind. She was okay with that. She needed to say it. The planets were aligned for her when he said he not only believed her but he forgave her. That had been a weight that she was done carrying. She no longer had to hope and pray that he would say those words.

Even though she was an utter screw up who would most likely lose her license as an attorney and possibly be in jail for some time, tonight was a thank you from her to the universe for letting her have her evening with Carlos. She tried to focus on the gate opening which would mean he entered a code that still worked. Instead, her eyes followed his long, purposeful strides in denim jeans that fit every part of him perfectly from his taut behind to his powerful legs.

She shivered remembering what it felt like to have her legs wrapped snug around his hips as he made sweet love to her over and over. She would give anything to return to a moment like that again. Her reality was that now was not the time to have such thoughts. She was lucky that he no longer avoided her.

Her eyes stayed on Carlos as he pulled out his phone, most likely, in search of the passcode. She remembered him doing that several times in the past when they came up this road. When the gate slid open, she did a happy dance in her seat as Carlos walked back toward the car and got in with a smile of success.

"I guess today is your lucky day," she exclaimed as the car entered through the gate. Carlos waited until it had closed behind them before he took off up the short dirt road before the black pavement took them the rest of the way.

"That's true. I wasn't sure I still had the code in my phone."

Everly looked over at the only house beyond the gate. It was where Mr. Wally lived. Before they got too far, the light on the front porch came on, as it always had when they rolled by. That was due to one of many motion detectors on the property. In what was a moment of remembrance, Carlos lowered the window and waved, followed by a thumbs up. When a light inside of the house blinked on and off three times, she clapped like a kid in a candy store.

"He's still here! I was hoping. You haven't talked to him?"

"Not in about six months. He had a business meeting here about six months ago. I handled security for that gathering for him."

"Really? Do you know what kind of business he's in or is that still a mystery?"

Carlos nodded as they drove on. That was always a thing between him and Mr. Wally. They were friends who kept the mystery of their personal lives out of their friendship.

"He enjoys the life of a recluse. Seven months ago, I get a call, surprisingly, because I didn't remember giving him my cell number. He asked me to come up the mountain for a chat. He used to be the president of a bank. When his wife passed away, he retired to this property. He'd purchased it many years ago when he and his wife used to take a drive, just like us, to the summit to get away from the world. When she got sick, he moved them here where he took care of her with the help of a private healthcare company. He made the property secure and chose to live in solitude. As you know, I used to come up here for my runs. That was right around the time that he had the property enclosed, blocking off all access without his permission. We would talk whenever I came up here. I remember telling him about you. He said if I ever wanted to take you someplace nice and quiet, away from the world, I should take the road on the side of the house until it comes to a large open piece of land on the edge of the mountain. That used to be his spot with his wife. It then became my spot with you."

They were having a moment. Everly loved that. This night couldn't be more perfect.

"He's mysterious, generous and very nice. I see the two of you still have your signal."

"Yeah. I wasn't sure he would remember me or us."

Everly looked over at Carlos as he drove with a burning question on the tip of her tongue.

"It's been that long since you've been up here?" she asked without really asking the question she wanted to ask.

Carlos smiled over at her before putting his eyes back on the darkened road. The only lights showing them the way were from the car. She remembered Carlos once telling her that Mr.

Wally hadn't added any additional lights because he didn't want them seen at night by those passing by on the road below. That would make them curious enough to venture up his mountain. He didn't want that. As in the past, the starry night was their beacon for direction.

"Everly, all you have to do is ask. The answer to the question you didn't ask is, no, I haven't been here and no, I haven't brought another woman up here. Too many memories live in my head with you and I being here."

"How long has your friend had this car? I've never seen a black Jaguar with money green interior. You were right about how dark the windows are. It sure is a beauty."

"I know. He's had it a few months. Once we secured the contracts with the two casinos and the mayor's office, I moved him up the chain to my first vice president of operations and training. I gave him a huge signing bonus to help me run things and conduct the training of new team members. This was his first purchase after moving his mother into the house of her dreams in Florida where he's from. He doesn't drive it often. He also has a Navigator truck. He and his wife have four kids. They need cars with room. The jaguar is his car when he needs to show and prove who he didn't want to forget he was before marriage and kids. He keeps it in a secure location in the garage at the casino. Anyone entering that area has to have a special code, just like we used to get up here on the summit."

"Thanks for getting me outside tonight. I've only been out during the day to go to court."

"You're welcome. I could use the night air myself."

"Do you still go on long, late-night drives to clear your head; to think?"

"I do it every chance I get. The casinos and other business responsibilities keep me pretty busy, so I don't get out for downtime as often as I would like. When I do, I never thought to come up here."

Everly was about to question why when the hill opened up into a large flat surface. Carlos stopped the car and they turned to each other with the same look of surprise on their faces. Their spot was different. Mr. Wally had added, what looked like a love nest built into the side of the mountain overlooking the expanse of Chicago below.

"What is this? Wow!" Everly exclaimed.

"What the hell?" Carlos added as his eyes took in exactly what she saw. He was mesmerized by the sight before them. Stunned, he couldn't drive any further.

"Drive. I want a closer look," she said happily, tapping him on the arm.

Carlos nodded and slowly moved the car forward. The minute they exited the roadway and pulled onto the flat surface, a light came on to illuminate the mountain top. Carlos pulled the car around until they were on the side of the new structure that looked like a glass enclosed hotel. They were allowed to see some of the inside because of the light at the top of the roadway.

"There lights up here; finally," Carlos noticed.

"I guess he got over his fear of any light being seen from below," Everly acknowledged.

"This is incredible. When did Mr. Wally have time to have something like this done? It looks like a room actually built inside of the mountain," Carlos acknowledged.

"This reminds me of that trip we took to Los Angeles when we drove up Pacific Coast Highway into Malibu. Those houses looked wild built into the side of a large rock. That's what this is like. It's beautiful. Should we get out?" Everly asked.

"I guess we should. I know we were coming up for a ride to look at the view from the car, but this is too good to not take a look at."

Carlos turned the car off and walked around to help Everly get out. Before they left the casino hotel, she'd changed out of her dress and heels and put on a fleece sweat suit that had a short skirt instead of sweatpants. He loved her in the orange and white outfit with matching sneakers with an orange stripe.

He started to grab the bags of food, but decided to wait until they were done checking everything out.

"Carlos, this is beyond words. Look, there is a large box on the side of the glass enclosure. It looks like there is an envelope inside."

They walked hand-in-hand to check it out. Everly was about to ask even more questions about the box and the envelope inside when Carlos noted a sign on the wall above the box.

"Your code will open this piece of heaven," Carlos read.

Again, they looked to each other trying to understand what was happening. Mister Wally had been full of surprises from the moment they'd all met. He blew their mind with how much he knew about them.

"Well?" she asked, pointing to the keypad. "We've come this far. This feels like one of those mystery rooms where you get to the next level with each clue."

"Let's see what's next."

After putting his code into the keypad, the box clicked and the lid opened like a safe door. He reached in and took out the envelope inside. Everly had moved forward around toward the front of the enclosure.

"I think there is a door on the other side," she said.

"Wait. I need you to listen to this," Carlos said, stopping her in her tracks. "I saw the news that your lady was back. I don't know what happened and I don't care. I do know that something happened when you stopped coming up the mountain. I've made some changes that I hope you'll enjoy. If you two are anything like my wife and I were, it gets old making love in the back seat of a car. It also gets cold up here trying to make love and be comfortable on a blanket this high up. If you two find your way back to each other and you make it back to your spot, this upgrade is for you. There is electricity and running water. I've had it aired out and cleaned every Saturday for the past three months since the project was complete. This is a place that you can come to and you don't have to go back down the mountain if you're tired. There is state of the art everything inside. The best part is that on one side, you can still see the Chicago sky view, the most beautiful view in the world. It's signed, Mr. Wally."

Everly gasped as she tried to look inside.

"He did this thinking we would get back to the summit together? I can't believe it."

"Me either," Carlos said, realizing what being up on the mountain meant. He wasn't sure they should go inside. The possibility of what that meant isn't why he brought her up the mountain.

"You're thinking we shouldn't go inside?" she asked.

"I don't know what I'm thinking. Everly, I didn't bring you up here for this. I hope you're not thinking that."

"I don't know what I'm thinking other than I want to see what's inside. He built this for us. I mean, I know there's no us, but still, he built this for us. Aren't you curious?" she asked.

Walking around the large glass enclosure to get to the other side, Carlos walked up to the large steal door and again, entered the code. The door clicked and opened. Looking inside, the area was completely lit up. Everly grabbed his hand from behind and held on tight as they entered.

"This is something. There is an entryway, a large bathroom and an extremely large bedroom," he noted.

"The bed overlooks the mountain. It's so beautiful and fresh smelling. I can't even begin to imagine the upkeep let alone the building of this and adding electricity. Did you know Mr. Wally was rich?" Everly asked.

"Not until I did security for him at his meeting. The people he had present were some of the richest men in the country. I never expected anything like this. It definitely protects from the elements. Remember all of the mosquito bites all over our bodies after making love outside under the moon and stars?" Carlos questioned. Even if she wasn't thinking about it, he certainly was. Neither of them had cared about bug bites. They made love outside under the stars and yelped at the moon like wild animals in heat because they were.

"How could I forget. I never regretted even a single bite."

Everly walked into the bedroom and right up to the large thick paned window.

"Beautiful," Carlos said in a low tone.

"It sure is."

"I'm not talking about that view."

Everly closed her eyes without turning around and wrapped her head around where her head was. She thought he was talking about the view outside of the window like she was. If it wasn't for the immediate sizzle that seared through her body at the deep, sexual tone of his words, she would have overlooked what or who he was focused on; that would be her. She turned and leaned back against the glass finding Carlos standing in the doorway, hands behind his back, his eyes taking in all of her.

"I love this place. It's the most romantic setting I've ever been in and you've taken me to a few very nice places before. This one is special because it's built on the place that was just for you and me. I'm feeling some sort of way."

"Oh? Tell me about that," Carlos said and closed the gap between them.

"I can't."

"Why not?"

"Because I don't want to assume you feel the same way."

"You won't know unless you share."

"It's this place, Carlos."

"Is it? What about earlier?"

"Earlier?"

"At my place. I needed to get out of there because every time I looked at you, all I could think about was sinking inside of you. Even after all that has happened, I still have that on my mind when I see you. It's why I tried avoiding you. I thought coming up here, we would take a drive, see the view and get back to the hotel because we both need to get up early; you for court and me for three business meetings I have."

"And then you saw this place."

Carlos shook his head no. It wasn't just this place.

"And then I saw you in this place."

Seeing Carlos' steaming gaze on her was a stroll down a sexy memory lane. That look always told her what he wanted and back then, what he needed. An immediate craving between her legs stirred to life. It was a feeling she hadn't experienced in a long time. She knew the moment she'd left Chicago for parts unknown under duress, she would not let another man touch her that wasn't him until she knew for a fact that there could never be anything between them again. What she was seeing all over him right now spoke volumes. They weren't done with each other yet.

In the quiet of the space, Everly could hear her own ragged breaths and feel her rapid beating heart. If only she could really have him. It's been so long.

"I see you here too. Is that wrong of me?"

He didn't answer her. Instead, she fidgeted nervously as his slow, methodical steps brought him right in front of her. Being chest height to him, she slowing moved her eyes up his body to his hooded gaze. Instead of his eyes being locked on her eyes, his were focused on her lips. Hoping that she could have one more, just one more touch of his lips to hers, she prepared hers for his. She watched his eyes focus on her as she slowly stuck her tongue out and licked across the strawberry flavored gloss she'd applied.

"There is nothing wrong about this place or what you see. I know that for a fact from my end. I have a lot of memories when it comes to the summit. All the times we..."

"I know. I've been thinking about that from the moment you mentioned taking a drive here."

"Everly, I want you. At the same time, I shouldn't want you. I'm trying to figure out what that conflict within me means. I was crushed when you left me. We were perfect together in every way, especially an intimate one. The lust for each other had no boundaries. You're back. You're here. We're here in this space. It's more romantic than it's ever been. There is no doubt about that. I don't want to misconstrue what I'm feeling. Could I feel like this here in this space for anyone else? Absolutely not. Should I feel this want for you in this space? Probably not. Can I flip it off as if it doesn't exist? Hell no."

"Carlos, I know that I will forever want you."

"You are so damn gorgeous. Still, you get a rise out of me; rocky past and all. Digesting if wanting you is for now, at this given moment. Is it beyond right now? I don't know what I would offer you. Things, other than my carnal desire for you, are still up in the air. Until everything is resolved, I am here tonight."

"So am I. I wouldn't ask you for anything, considering I probably don't even deserve the help you're giving me now. To want me? I am excited about that. My body is going crazy with the idea of that. Not having intimacy in a year is mind blowing. Not wanting it from anyone else but you, is the prison I've put myself in because I've only wanted to belong to you. If you say that I can have you tonight and only tonight, I want that. I need that. I forever be happy because I had the chance to see what Mr. Wally did especially knowing he had us in mind. If I never get to be in this place with you again after today, I'm okay with that. I have right now. What we do with right now? I'm leaving that up to you. I'm okay with one night only."

To prove she mean it, Everly reached for the zipper of the top of her sweat suit and slid it down until it opened and gaped enough for Carlos to get an eyeful. The moment she knew he had, she smiled to herself. This wasn't a trick or treachery.

This was her, hopefully, getting a night of love from the only man she's ever loved. When he didn't make a move, she didn't know if she should go further. To issue a field test, she attempted to slide the zipper back up when Carlos' hand stopped her. He gripped the zipper and slid it back down until the sides fell away. When his hands made contact with her waist, she exhaled an exhilarating sigh that she was feeling his touch again.

"One night? Is that enough for you?" Carlos asked.

"Never, but if that's all you can offer me, one night is what I'll take."

No further words. Everly's head exploded with delight when Carlos leaned down and kissed her. It wasn't one of those soft, pliant or easily charming kisses. Even if she was kidding herself, she felt like the kiss spoke to how much he missed her. When he pulled back, clearly to catch his breath after stealing hers right out of her mouth, she needed more.

Grabbing Carlos by his shirt, she pulled him back in for another heated exchange and this time, pressing seductively into his mouth, she deepened the kiss, taking control. When she felt herself being lifted into the air, she moved her hands to his shoulders. Nothing prepared her for his next move. They kissed. She heard his belt buckle opening. They kissed more. She heard his zipper going down. Her head was having a dance party. She was thankful that she had on a dress. There was no need for any pretense. She didn't need any. With him, she never did. Her legs were wide open and wrapped around his waist. She felt him at her entrance. Inwardly she screamed yes, over and over again. His fingers found their way to her steamy center. He never made love to her without making sure her body was ready for him.

"You're already dripping wet," he whispered in her ear as his fingers played in the moisture he found there.

"From the moment you looked at me from the doorway. I hopeful and ready."

"Ready is good," was all Carlos said

His erection easily slid inside of her.

"Oh," she screamed loudly, her sensual response echoed against the glass walls around them.

"Tight," Carlos commented.

Everly looked into his handsome face and saw that he was clearly restraining himself from going in all the way. It had been a year for her. She expected some tightness. That may be how he felt it but to her, she needed more.

"More," she uttered against his lips.

"Mmm, explain more," he replied, kissing her deeply again before she could reply.

She did, but now with words. She used her body.

Braced against the glass, with his legs holding her up, she moved up until he slid part way out of her body. With only the tip in, she moved back down, taking more and more of him with each rise and fall on him.

Carlos then forged a pace that sent a clear message of lust and desire that had gone unfulfilled between them for far too long. They were perfect together. She felt at home surrounding that part of him that brought sheer delight throughout her body.

With his powerful legs coming into play, Carlos grunted with each surge up into her body, taking her hands into his and placing them against the glass with the back of her hand feeling the coldness. It was the only part of her that had the slightest chill. Heat fused where their bodies met.

When he increased the pace, she rode him and accepted every stroke like a starving woman. Wishing that the feeling could last much longer than her body was about to tell her wasn't to be, meeting him thrust for thrust, her climactic point ripped through her with a fiery fierceness that took her breath away. Carlos increased the pace and prolonged the amazing feelings flowing through her body. In the next moment, she felt Carlos surrender to his own release, increasing the pace of his pulses into her body to a frenetic speed until his head flew back and he howled into the night. They had exploded together over and over again until the feeling crested and set them free.

They stayed in the position against the window until Carlos held her tighter and moved them to the bed. He laid on his back and pulled her on top of him. He kissed her face and then her neck; both continued to find their breath again.

She kicked herself when he pulled her snug against him. She told him that she was okay with this one time tonight. She had lied. One was not going to be enough for her. Not now, not ever.

12

The only thought running through Carlos' mind was that getting out of his bed at an ungodly hour on his day off to meet with a man he wanted and needed to despise had better be worth what he left behind in his bed.

After their trek up to the summit over a week ago, he tried staying away from Everly. After three days, he failed at that miserable. He refused to admit that he missed her. Knowing she'd had a meeting with her attorney that had not gone well during a day when they were texting, he called to be a place of peace when she was in a state of panic. They were equally concerned that without more proof about the major role Hamilton played, she was potentially looking at some major time. The prosecutors were playing hard ball with her. He wanted Everly to remain hopeful. He was certainly trying to be. He was already getting attached beyond where he wanted to be. The last thing he wanted was for her to be behind bars. That solitude would kill her. He wasn't sure how he would survive knowing that's where she would spend a lot of her years.

More than that, he'd been fighting his desire to be inside of her again after saying he could only give her that one night. Before they left the summit, he'd made love to her two more times before they finally showered and headed back down the mountain sometime in the middle of the night.

For the past few nights, Everly had spent them with him. When he had to work late, he enjoyed coming to his suite to find here still there. They had taken their pleasure with each other day and night. She had more meetings coming up before a court date in three weeks. He wanted to take the sting of the possibility of what the future might look like for her away by spending time together that distracted her from her woes. The meeting this morning was an important one.

Carlos arrived in front of the elevator on his floor and inserted his personal code which called the elevator to the secure level where his suite was located. He could hear the sounds of it rising to pick him up. Looking back down the hall from where he'd come, he thought about Everly who was still sound asleep in his bed. He'd left her snuggled up under, not just the blankets but two pillows. Smiling, his mind took him back to a time in their relationship when he asked her about that. She told him it was a sign that she was sleeping good. That was good information because they had talked the evening before about how she hadn't been getting much sleep since her world had come crashing down around her.

Being in his bed with her was exactly where he wanted to be. That was until a member of his security team, Boone, called to let him know he had a visitor. Initially, he told him that anyone looking to speak with him needed to make an appointment. There was someone in charge on his day off who could handle everything else. Just when he was about to hang up, Boone finally coughed up who the visitor was. It was Nathaniel Briggs, Hamilton's father. The fact that the man was at the casino was enough for him to slip out from his position of his naked body being half-covered by Everly's perfectly sculpted nakedness. Only curiosity got him up, dressed and stepping into the elevator. He'd left Everly a note letting her know that he had something to take care of but hoped that she would stay put until he returned. He made no reference to his leaving to meet Nathaniel. He didn't know how long he would be. What he did know was that if he could get back to the room to find her in the same position she was in when he'd left, he would be in a rush to undress and get back in bed.

The elevator stopped on the second floor of the casino where the business offices were. He'd had Boone place Nathaniel into the conference room with an instruction to keep a close eye on him. Knowing who his son was, Carlos wasn't sure his father could be trusted. He wondered if it was possible that he knew Everly was there. If that was the case, he would beef up security around her in the hotel. He had already expected his team to keep an eye out for anyone referencing her in conversations around the hotel and casino. If need be, he would move her into his suite until the crisis was over. Continuing to post security outside of her room would work, but he felt better knowing no one could get to her in his suite.

His long strides made haste as he looked to his left the minute the inside of the conference came into view. Sure enough, pacing nervously with his hands in the pockets of his pants was Hamilton's father. He walked past one of the females on his team, Olivia, who stood outside the conference room door. He whispered to her to be ready to toss the man out if the conversation went left. Entering, he found Boone keeping his eyes on every step Nathaniel took.

"Boss," Boone said when he entered.

"Carlos," Nathaniel acknowledged.

"Mr. Briggs," Carlos offered.

"You usually call me Mr. Nat or Nathaniel."

"True. That was until I realized I don't know how to feel about the Briggs family yet. I hope you can give me a reason to call you Mr. Nat again."

Carlos walked closer as the man extended his hand. Usually, he wouldn't leave a hand un-shook, but today, he wasn't in the mood. Too much was tied up into a big ball of confusion. That meant, for the moment, no one with the last name of Briggs was to be trusted.

Nathaniel looked around the room, then to Boone and then to him.

"Do you think we can speak alone?" he asked.

"Not today we can't. Boone stays. It's seven in the morning. You woke me from some much-needed sleep. The hours of running the security for a casino are long. This conversation had better be enlightening. For starters, where is Ham?"

"Do you mind if I sit down?" Nathaniel asked.

Carlos extended his hand and pointed to a seat. He chose to stand. Moving to a spot against the glass wall of the room, he crossed his hands in front of him and waited.

"Where's Ham?" he asked a second time.

"So, you know what's going on?"

"How could I not. It's the biggest news story since the Bernie Madoff story out of New York some years ago. Yeah, I'm up to speed."

"Do you know how Everly is doing?"

Hearing the man say her name place his internal radar on alert. He didn't like how the conversation was starting.

"Why? Are you hear trying to find out if I know where she is so that you can share that information with your son? I hear he may be back in Chicago. That's pretty risky considering every law enforcement agency is looking for him, according to the news."

"He's in a lot of trouble."

"I don't give a damn about the amount of trouble Ham is in. He's leaving a woman to take the fall for his criminal behavior. Might I add, what he did was done to *your* company. How could you not know what Ham was doing at your firm? I get it's a need-to-know situation and I'm far from the audience who needs to know. He came for her and now look where she is."

"So, you *do* know where she is? You've talked to her?"

"Mr. Briggs, change your questioning or I'm out of here," Carlos demanded.

He knew this wasn't going to go well. The man was making his point true.

"I genuinely want to know if she's okay. I'm not asking for my son."

"Whether I have or not isn't your concern. I'm not going to help you to help Ham harm her. If he is, in fact, back in Chicago, he's here for one reason only. He's here to make sure Everly doesn't spill all of the beans of what took place. I assume you're here for Ham's interest in all of this?"

"Carlos, I am not. You should know me better than that. Yes, he's my son, but he's done some terrible things that have impacted a lot of people. A few people whose life savings were stolen by my son have taken their own lives rather than live with having nothing to live off of now. I have family members who invested with my firm. Their money is gone too. My firm has been a trusted agency for a lot of years. I had no idea what Ham was doing."

"You should know that if he tries in any way, to hurt Everly, he will never get the chance to hurt anyone ever again. I will see to that. I stood by and watched him take her away from me one time. He won't be able to do it on any level a second time around. He's ruined her life. He's responsible if she loses her freedom. There is a good chance she will go to prison for a long time, especially if Ham is never found and brought to justice. He holds the answers."

"Everly holds some along with her father. They were all in on this together."

"No!" Carlos yelled.

"Boss?" Boone interrupted.

Carlos didn't raise his voice like that often. Hearing him do so had to have shocked Boone.

"I'm good."

"I get it, not Everly. A lot of what was done was at her expense. I get that now. I was approached by the Feds. From what I gather, I think they know Everly was manipulated. It doesn't make her totally innocent. I'm sorry for what he's done to her life."

"Ham isn't anything like who I thought he was. I knew we weren't the greatest of friends, but still, friends. He came for my woman and then intimidated her away from me by using her love for her brother and her love for me. He used my friendship with him to con my woman."

"Hamilton has always been jealous of you, Carlos. That's a given. Did you know that? I knew it a long time ago. He once cursed me for respecting you more than I respected him. Ham was never an honest, hardworking man like yourself. Oh, he's brilliant. He never learned how to use that for good. There has always been on scheme after another. I didn't think he would come for my company. You have always fought hard for where you are. I've always admired that about you. I had hoped some of who you are would rub off on my son. Instead, he spent his life figuring out how to skirt the system to make a name for himself. My relationship with him looked good on the surface but it wasn't. I took blame for the trouble he would often find himself in. I tried to make amends for not being the kind of supportive dad I should have been by bringing him into the firm. I was ecstatic when he went to college for finance with a strong desire to be in my world. I thought that we could build something together. I had no idea he was running a side game. Did you know about Everly's father's involvement in all of this?"

Carlos started to reply and then thought deeply about what had just been shared with him. As a Leo, he overthought everything including every word in a sentence, especially those that ended in a question mark.

"You've heard from Ham, haven't you? I've seen the news. I haven't seen anything mentioned about her father. They're looking for Hamilton because he worked for your firm. No one but him could have pulled this off without being noticed. There were protections in place to prevent this type of thing. Stealing money at that level took careful planning over a period of time. I don't quite get all that Everly's role was. Everything that has happened started with Ham and should end with him and not Everly. He's a coward."

"True. He's a coward that has returned to Chicago. Yes, he's looking for Everly."

Carlos moved and sat at the table across from him. His interest was on a new level. Something told him to watch Everly's six because he felt like Ham was somewhere watching her or trying to. The best idea he'd ever had was to bring her to the casino. The place was as secure as the White House.

"I will kill him if he even gets close enough to move one of her hairs out of place. Do you get that?" Carlos spoke harshly through clinched teeth with one finger pointing close to the man's face from opposite sides of the table.

Nathaniel exhaled loudly and put both of his hands in the air in surrender.

Carlos leaned back in his chair. He wiped his hand down his face and across his chin in order to calm down.

"I'm here because I don't want that. I know you may find this hard to believe but I want my son to stand in judgement for his crimes."

"Are you sure you're not here to protect yourself and your company? I'm not sure I can get behind the idea that you want to see Ham in prison."

"In place of that young woman? Absolutely. I came to you because I can't go to her. I know that she's heavily protected. When I first heard that Everly had left the country with Ham, I was shocked. The two of you were and probably still are perfect for each other. I watched how you looked at each other the few times Ham had the two of you to our house for one event or another. I was shocked when things ended between you to then find she was with Ham. I didn't see that coming. What does he have on her besides what he's done with stealing the money? He had to have something on her to get her away from you. She loved you. Anyone who knew you two knew that. It was written as clear as day in the sky."

Carlos still wasn't sure he trusted the man. He wanted to find a way to get Everly off the hook. She may not be able to walk away without any charges but bringing in Ham and possibly her father would go a long way with the court.

"Why are you here? What do you want from me?"

"I want to bring in Ham before he gets himself killed either by you or the Feds. He won't turn himself in. He knows if he's caught, he will never see the outside of a jail cell for the rest of his life. To say that he is unhinged is an understatement."

"He reached out to you. What did he say?"

"He wants me to find out where Everly is. He promised me that he would return the money, or at least what's left over if I can find out where Everly is. She's the only witness they have who could bury him. I know what that means. No, I don't want that for her. I wouldn't want that for anyone. I want my son brought in alive to stand trial for what he's done. People deserve to get their money back."

"Why haven't you gone to the feds with what you know, especially about being contacted by Ham?"

"Believe this or not but I want to protect Everly. Telling them about Ham won't help her. Your lady does not deserve any of this. Ham has a lot of wires loose right now. He's desperate. He told me she got away from him. He lost it when he saw her on television after turning herself in. Being betrayed is something he can dish out but not take from someone else. I don't know what went on between him and Everly, but..."

"Nothing," Carlos interrupted. "Nothing at all. I know what you're thinking. It wasn't what I thought it was or what he wanted it to be."

"Everly told you that?"

Carlos paused. He has yet to say that he has spoken to Everly. He wasn't one hundred percent sure he was ready to share what he knew but like Nathaniel, he wanted to protect Everly. He decided to go with his first instinct. He's never had a real reason to not trust Ham's father even though his son was the worst of the worst.

"She did. He held her brother's life over her head. They did not have a romantic involvement, though he made it clear he wanted that."

"I told you that he's always been jealous of you. I don't know why. My wife and I gave him everything. Perhaps we didn't give him the love and attention he needed growing up. I don't know. Does anybody know what makes someone do the things that they do when it comes to committing guilt-free crimes? I wouldn't know how to help him other than to get him in safely. I need to do that. I need your help."

"Oh? Why?"

"I think he knows Everly came back here to come to you for help. According to him, while she was with him, she talked about how much she missed you and loved you. She beat herself up over what you must have thought about her. He said she did what she did to protect you from her father's wrath."

"Her father is a dangerous man; more dangerous than Ham could ever be. At least that's what I thought before hearing that he's here after Everly. He won't get to her. My team is protecting her; not just the feds. They know what to do if Ham shows up."

"How can we avoid that and still bring him in? I think you're the key."

"Me?"

"He's always tried to compete with you and your popularity. I'm not talking about with women, but with people in general. He had to work hard at being liked. He used to say that people would flock to you without you making a play for their attention. Ham had to go an extra step to be that type of person. That was something he hated. Being your friend wasn't fake. I believe he stayed close until the day came when he could say he beat you on something; anything. Being truthful, he has also always had the utmost respect and admiration for you. Ham asked for my help in hiding him. The heat is on. He knows I'm being watched assuming he would reach to me first. He did so through a friend who brought his phone to me with a call from Ham. I agreed to meet him on the pier. Most of all, he wants me to tell him where Everly is."

"He won't be able to get to her."

"I know that. I knew she would come to you. I also knew that no one, even after what they did to you, no one would look after her like you would. I'm happy knowing she is safe. Money can buy a lot of people, which is what I think Ham is trying to do. You, however, will never be for sale for any amount. I want my son safe. I need you to talk to him. Can you do that?"

"Why not tell the feds where he'll be? They can bring him in without incident."

"What if something happens? He has a hit out on Everly. He's trying to get to her himself, but he knows the feds are keeping her close. They may bring him in but that won't stop the hit on Everly. I believe only you can talk him off of the ledge. Can I ask that you at least think about it?"

"When are you meeting him?"

"In a few days as long as I can get your help. I know he will listen to you. Over me, he will listen to you."

"I don't know what to say to him. I'm not level headed right now either."

"But you would do anything to protect Everly. I'm telling you she is in danger. Whatever you are doing to protect her, keep doing it. I don't know who he's hired. I understand some of the men searching for her were sent by her father. Did you know that her father killed her mother when she was a child? He did that and then left his kids to fend for themselves in the system. Ham told me that before Everly was able to get away from them, her father's plan was to kill her but his girlfriend helped Everly escape. That woman is now dead. Her father did to her what he did to Everly's mother, leaving another little girl without her mother."

Carlos couldn't believe what he was hearing. Everly mentioned having a little sister when they talked.

"My god! What is Ham thinking getting wrapped up in a man like that? One of Everly's friends was ferociously attacked in New York. That has either Ham or her father written all over it. He has to be stopped. I agree with you on that. Killing women? I don't even know how to tell Everly about that. Someone out there is her sister. She's going to want help finding her. This is a lot to take in," Carlos said.

After her friend Cecily being beat up and now her sister being left alone, Everly couldn't catch a break. Nathaniel was right. The only end to this was either Everly getting killed, Hamilton getting killed or having him come in safely. Hamilton did him wrong but despite what's he's done, in his heart, he didn't want to see him dead. He'd like to be alone in a room with him for a few hours to work out his frustration on his face, but he'll digress and let that be.

Carlos stood to leave. Nathaniel stood with him.

"Give me a few days. In the meantime, reach to Ham and let him know that you've found Everly and that you're going to bring her to him. I'll be there. She won't. I don't want her anywhere around however this turns out. Don't contact me directly. Call the casino office. Boone here will give you a number to call. They'll get a message to me. Let me know where we're meeting. You should know, I legally carry a weapon. I will have it with me. How things turn out will be up to you and your son."

Nathaniel nodded.

"I understand. After all that he's done to you and Everly, I thank you for still having a heart kind enough to help me keep my son alive."

Carlos nodded and when Nathaniel held his hand out this time, he shook it. He left the room, leaving the man behind. He wasn't going directly back to Everly. He needed to think. First of all, he needed to talk to a few members of his team who could keep a secret. Most of all, he needed Melvin. He would send a replacement for him to continue looking after Cecily. He only trusted Melvin to have his back. Ham and Everly's father are out of control. He trusted no one; especially not a man who pretended to be his friend only to ruin his life and that of a woman Ham knew he loved. Truth is, he still does.

13

Everly heard the suite door open over the soft music playing through the speakers built into the wall of the bathroom. She closed her eyes and thought back to the night before and smiled hoping that Carlos would be happy that she had stayed around and waited for him. How long she'd been asleep after he left out, she didn't know.

After one of the best nights of sleep that she's had in a long time, she woke and stretched. When she reached across the bed and her hands didn't find him next to her, she shot right up and out of the bed. On instinct, she grabbed her dress from the floor next to the bed where Carlos had tossed after picking her up and carrying her to bed. They had been relaxing until he looked over at her from the opposite end of the sofa. No words were exchanged. They were thinking the exact same thing. That was, the television show they were watching could wait.

Looking throughout his two-bedroom suite, she rushed back into the bedroom. That's when she found the note he'd left for her. It must have fallen from the night stand to the floor where she found it. Knowing he wanted her to stay delighted her. She didn't want to live on the border of false hope that incredible sex between them three times in one night would mean that they were back together. What she never forgot was Carlos' libido. The soreness between her legs when she woke up reminded her of how much she missed how wild they could be together. For her, the wilder the better. Telling him a week ago that she hadn't been with anyone else since him seemed to drive him even wilder and more ferocious on the sexiest level possible every time they were together since that first night up the mountain. The way she loved him before, and still did, no way matched her desire for him last night. She thought she would be jealous when he admitted that he hadn't been without having a woman in his bed after she left him. Her expectation was never that. To be with him again was all she could ask for.

Soaking in the hot bath was exactly what her body and mind needed. Waking up in Carlos' bed was a shock to her system. It wasn't about the location as much as it was about not being able to sleep peacefully in months; pretty much close to a year which meant the entire time she's spent apart from him. After making love the last time, they had passed out from sexual exhaustion; definitely a good thing. The only reason she could think of for her good night's sleep was because of how safe she felt with Carlos.

Leaning back, she waited until he looked around to finally find her relaxing in a tub full of bubbles.

"Should I even ask where you got bubbles from? I know there is nothing in my suite that would make that many of them, let alone with the scent of lavender and vanilla."

Before she could answer, Carlos walked over, leaned down and kissed her so thoroughly that her body reacted in a way that made her ready to jumped out of it and on him. She moaned into his mouth when his hand slipped below the bubbles and palmed one of her breasts, holding it firmly in his large hands, caressing her nipple until it pebbled to a point. She laughed when he pulled his hand out, stood and wiped the bubbles from his hand across her chin.

"Don't be mad."

"Mad? What? About that fact that the guy I placed outside of the room while I was gone walked you to your room to get what you needed? Bubbles and all?"

Her heart melted when he hit her with his thousand-watt smile.

"You know about that?"

"He texted me as soon as you asked him if he could walk you there and back."

"I didn't see him do that."

"You weren't supposed to. Not letting you out of his sight meant just that. You're not a prisoner here. My people have the highest of security clearance. He wouldn't hesitate to escort you as long as he protected every little step you took."

"Oh, that's good. I don't want anyone in any trouble. You told me no slipping away and I didn't want to do that. I did, however, need to freshen up. I started to take a bath in my room."

"I'm glad you didn't. Thinking of what those bubbles are hiding from me is titillating. Did you get everything you needed from your room?"

"Toiletries and a change of clothes. We came right back here. I will admit that I didn't think anyone was outside the door. I was going to race to my room and get back before you knew I had left out. Then I realized I wouldn't be able to get back up here if I tried that. I called the number you left me on the note that said if I needed anything to dial that number only. The woman who answered said that someone was outside of the door. She had me check to be sure. I did. She said to check with him if I needed anything."

"He checked with me."

"I wasn't sure he would do that."

"Hmph. He knows better. He likes being employed. Most of all, he enjoys the large pay check."

"I'm assuming he also didn't want to have to deal with you. I love a powerful man."

The moment the words left her mouth, Everly wished she could retrieve them. She was getting too comfortable too fast. It wasn't that she didn't want to. The issue was, she didn't want to push him back into something with her that he wasn't looking for. He was helping her out. They'd had fun. She didn't want to push or cross a line that would make him uncomfortable. Hoping he didn't focus on her slip-up, she moved her hand across the bubbles.

"Smells great in here," Carlos said letting her off the hook.

"Your sister gave me this bubble bath and accompanying bath bombs. She said she's releasing her own line of bath products, including a sensually stimulating line for women. The pheromones are secreted scents that give off a carnal signal from within the same species."

"Is that so? Well, it may be working because I'm thinking about joining you in that tub. Do you know you're the only woman who has ever been able to get me in a tub? I'm usually strictly a shower type of guy."

"Oh, please. You never got in the tub with me to take a bath. You got in because you loved having sex in the tub. You love sex in the water."

"And you know this to be a fact."

Everly moved up a little, sitting straighter in the tub so that her breast bounced on top of the water. She wanted to give him an eyeful. Carlos loved the female body. Most of all, he was a breast man. She had quite a bit for him to caress with his eyes. Teasing him, she moved her hands across her breasts, allowing her fingers to caress both nipples until they were straining painfully hard at the thought of the number of times he sucked them into his mouth the night before.

"I can remember back when you had your braids. I do love the bald head, by the way. We were on a private beach in Fiji for five days. You made love to me in the ocean, on the sand, though on a towel, in the pool on the deck; just about every surface we could find. The way you loved me on that beach was out of this world. When you had me in that pool with my legs wrapped around your hips, your hands holding me to you, using them to guide me around you back and forth, I saw the epitome of perfect joy on your face every time you climaxed. You love sex in water. Do you know what I love about the tub in your suite?"

"I can't wait to hear it. Before you tell me, know this, I heard you say the word love before you looked away. Don't be shy around me. You never have been before and so don't do it now. I know things are different but I'm still Carlos. Don't hide anything from me."

She should have known that he'd heard her. Most of all, she didn't want to scare him away by revealing how she still felt about him. She didn't want to make it about the sex. It was definitely about the never-ending love she's always felt for him.

"I will never do that again; I promise. I mean, I'm not saying this is leading to anything other than you and your team escorting and protecting me and you and I enjoying some good sex. I don't want you to think that over the past, almost a year, that I stopped loving you. I never, ever stopped thinking about you. I know my excuse of doing what I needed to do to protect you and my brother didn't sit well with you, but it's the truth. In spite of what happened, I never stopped loving you. I don't want that to scare you off as if I have expectations of you. The life you lived while I was gone didn't stop because I'm back. I know what this is. I'm okay with it. I didn't think I'd be with you last night. Thank you for not tossing me out on my head. Thanks for not continuing to avoid me."

"Just don't hide from me. Don't keep things from me. Talk to me. That's all I can ask. It's also all I can offer right now. I don't know how else to say that. I am consistent with who I am."

"I'm not, right?"

Everly hated that she was labeling herself as unreliable. She deserved that.

"I'm not saying that. A lot has happened. Let's give each other a minute to deal with what the priority is. That is to keep you safe. Now, about why you love the tub?"

Carlos' sneaky smirk as his eyes traveled from her face to her breasts let her know that they were back to the sexy part of the conversation.

"I love that it's not only big enough for two people, even one as tall as you but there is room to actually move around a bit with two people in it; different positions if need be."

"More of last night?" he asked.

"Much more if that's okay with you. I know you're a busy man. I don't want to keep you from anything."

"Baby, right now the only thing keeping me from anything is that I'm fully clothed. I'm about to remedy that. First, I need to talk to you."

Carlos leaned against the long edge of the his and her sink and crossed his legs at the ankles.

"Do you need me to get out?" she asked.

He was being very serious. His mood quickly turned deep. She even saw a hint of sadness.

"Don't you dare. Like I said, I'm definitely planning on joining you. I have an open day and most of the evening. I'm going to do a casino check with several members of my team around midnight but until then, you have my undivided attention unless something comes up."

"Like this morning?" she asked.

"That's what I want to talk to you about. My phone buzzed several times on the nightstand early this morning. It was a member of my team alerting me that I had a visitor in the casino."

Everly thought about the woman she'd seen him with and wondered if it was her.

"Oh?"

"Yes. It was Nathaniel Briggs, Ham's father."

Her ears and her eyes perked up.

"What? Here at the casino? He knows I'm here? Does Hamilton know?"

Everly was uncomfortable. What did this mean? Was she in danger? Was she putting Carlos in danger?

Carlos walked over and sat on the edge of the tub. He took her hand in his. He had seen her nervousness.

"Nathaniel knows that I know where you are but I didn't tell him your location. He wanted to speak to me about keeping you safe despite the fact that Hamilton wants otherwise."

"Hamilton *is* back then. That really was him that hurt Cecily."

"It was him; that is a given. That happened in New York. I had no doubt he was looking for you. If you weren't there then he must have known you had to be here in Chicago, perhaps with me."

"Carlos, I don't want to put you in danger. I'm sure the feds will put me someplace safe. Hamilton may not be as dangerous as my father but what was done to Cecily was more than just him. That was no doubt my father having some of his men do that. I can't see Hamilton beating up a woman. I can see him being there knowing it was happening, but striking a blow? I'm not so sure."

"Either way, he is here in Chicago and looking for you. His father believes there is a hit out on your life by him and possibly your father. They want to silence you about what you know. Even though there is no doubt he stole the money, what occurred after that no one else knows but you."

"His father cares about keeping me safe?"

"More than that, he wanted to be sure that Hamilton doesn't continue to slip and fall in his own way where he could possibly end up dead. I would see to that myself if he lays a hand on you himself or through anyone. His father wants him to turn himself in and deal with the consequences. Most of all, return the money he stole."

"They won't get all of that back. Most of it went into my father's hands. He set all of this up with Hamilton. He used me to help them knowing I was a lawyer and could take steps that would be unseen. I regret the day I took the bar. I never want to practice law again. I probably won't be able to anyway once I go to prison."

"You're not going to prison. I'm going to have faith in your lawyer that she can get this all worked out. One way to do that would be to get Ham to turn himself in. That's where I come in, according to his father."

"Is that so? How is that? What role is he asking you to play?"

"He wants me to meet with Ham and talk him off the ledge. He believes that there isn't another person on this earth that could talk to him that he would listen to. Can you believe that?"

"I can. Hamilton is so jealous of you that he couldn't stand his own self. He got a rise out of pulling me away from you. He never wanted you to know that it was all a farce and that we weren't romantically involved. He wanted the idea of that to eat away at you. He wanted to feel like he'd beat you at something; at what was most important in your life at that time outside of your family. He wanted me by any means necessary. I wouldn't give him me and so he was happy with what I could do to help him and my father financially."

"Listen, I have to tell you something and it's not good. Just hear me out, okay?"

"Carlos? With that look on your face, I'm scared."

Everly could feel her heart beat speed up, bouncing against the inside wall of her chest. She wasn't ready for any bad news.

"It's okay. I'm right here, okay?"

She nodded, unable to say yes.

"Is it Cecily? I haven't had a chance to talk to her. Is it her?" she asked.

"No. It's not about Cecily. I spoke with Melvin on my way back to the room. He said she's doing much better. He's on his way back to Chicago. If I'm going to meet with Ham, I'm going to need support. That will be Melvin. This is about the woman who helped you escape back to the U.S. Who was she?"

"Fancy. She was one of my father's girlfriends and the only one that had a child by him. I told you I have a baby sister. Her name is Ariel. When I ran, she took my sister and ran too. I was sad because I knew I would never see my sister again. I never see my brother and now that I have a sister, I will never see her again either. I don't have any family."

"That may be the case when it comes to blood relatives but you have all of us and your sister and your brother. There is a will and a way. It may take some time. I need to know everything about Fancy that you can think of."

"Are you going to try and find her? That could place her life in danger. She doesn't know anything more than what I know. In fact, I know more than she does."

"Well, that may be the case. The problem is, it appears, like with your mother, your father has killed Fancy."

Everly felt like the life had just left her body at the image in her head of the last time she'd seen Fancy. She was afraid but hopeful that she could get away and slip out of existence as far away from Arlo as possible.

"No!" she finally screamed. Covering her mouth, she held in the next scream though nothing could stop the tears from racing down her cheeks.

"I know. Like I said, I'm here. Let it out."

Everly's eyes widened at her next thought.

"My sister. Where is my sister? Did he hurt her too?" she asked, crying louder and harder.

"I don't know. That's why I need you to tell me about Fancy. Where would she have gone? Who did she know? From what Nathaniel said in what Hamilton told him, Arlo killed Fancy but not the baby. When I left him after we talked, he sent me a text to thank me for agreeing to help him with Ham. He also said that Ham noted that when Arlo's men caught up to Fancy, she didn't have her daughter with her. That means, she left her with someone."

Everly couldn't think straight. She wasn't aware of what Fancy's plans were to even know who she would have reached out to.

"I have to find her. She can't be alone in the world. I know what that feels like. I don't want that for her. She must be scared. She loved Fancy and Fancy made my sister her world. She was Fancy's reason for running away. How did my father find her? She was so sure she could safely get away."

"In that part of the country that is hard to do. She would have been safer if she'd found a way to get here to the U.S. like you did. I don't know much but I've got a few connections. I want to put some people on a trek to find her for you."

"You are?"

Everly cried harder.

"Please don't cry like this. My heart can't take seeing you like this."

"I'm sorry. You just stepped in without hesitation to help me and you haven't stopped. You don't have to look for my sister yet you know what that would mean to me. I need my sister."

"And she needs you. That's why I'm going to help Nathaniel convince Ham to come in before he gets killed. Who knows, your father may try and get rid of him. Anything is possible. I will do what I can."

Everly sniffled and Carlos handed her a hand towel to wipe her face. When she reached for it, he moved around her hand and wiped her eyes for her. She wanted to thank him but didn't get a chance. His lips finding hers was exactly what she needed.

The feel of him cleared her head and made her think good thoughts only. The kiss was tender as he kissed and nipped at her lips whispering against them that she didn't need to cry because he was here for her. She nodded as her lips desired more from his. Feeling his tongue seeking entrance into her mouth had her opening for him the same way that her heart was. She wanted to love him. She wanted him to love her. His mouth was telling her that he wanted her. She would take it even it if mean just for now.

The need to erase everything bad from this moment, Everly reached for the hem of Carlos' shirt and tried to pull it up and over his head without breaking the kiss for too long. Frustration settled in when she couldn't quite make it happen. She stopped tugging and ended the kiss.

"I don't want to talk anymore. Can we do that later? I know we need to talk and we will. Midnight will come sooner than I want it to. I want to focus on you for the rest of the day. You bring me peace. I need that more than I need to breathe right now. I also need to feel your arms around me. Please tell me I'm not asking for too much."

Her eyes locked with his as she looked for any sign that her request wasn't too much. Stepping back from the tub, her eyes focused on Carlos while he pulled his shirt up and off of his body before removing the rest of his clothes. When he stood naked and hard, her favorite, her mouth watered. Since it was only eleven in the morning, there would be time for more of what she really wanted to do to and for him. What she knew and loved about him was how much he enjoyed receiving oral pleasure as much as she loved giving it to him. If all she could get from him was today, there would be no wasting any of the day on talking when they could be making love until she passed out again.

14

Finally undressed, Carlos walked over to the tub, seeing the gleam in Everly's eyes as that part of him that he enjoyed sliding into her body stiffened at the pointed awareness that she was close by. He never had a problem being turned on by a beautiful woman, but there was something different and well aware when it came to being close to Everly. With all the women he's been with over the years, it wasn't just his body that proved that she was different, but his heart had fallen for her once again. That was a feeling no other woman had ever given him.

When she moved forward making room for him behind her, he moved his long legs into place on either side of her before leaning back. Placing his left arm along the white marble edge, he used the other to pull her snug against his hard body. Everly wiggled her hips and winked over her shoulder at him. After moving her long hair to one side, he placed a soft kiss in the center of her exposed neck.

"You added work to your tattoo," he noted, running his tongue along the edge of the red heart at the base of her hairline.

"I went with Fancy one day to this little shop. She wanted to get a tattoo with my sister's name on it. I...I..."

He heard her hesitancy in sharing more. Not sure why, he didn't want to intrude on what was holding her back from finishing. He caressed it with his hand hoping to soothe whatever had made her uncomfortable with sharing. He leaned forward and placed his head in the space between her head and her shoulder. He spoke softly.

"We've made love several times since you've been back. We're naked in a tub. I'm hard enough to break through a brick wall with my erection. Trust me when I say, at this time, there isn't a reason to hold anything from me. Whatever you were going to say, say it," he encouraged.

Everly turned her head to him, inhaled sharply and exhaled, allowing her body to relax.

"I feel you," she said, her hand reaching back between them to stroke him to an even more steely state of arousal.

"I know you do. In a few minutes, I can't wait for you to feel even more of me deep, deep inside of you. I know you trust me with your body. Do you trust me in every way?"

"Of course. With everything."

"Tell me what you didn't finish saying."

"I loved the red heart. As I waited for Fancy to be done, I saw a picture of a heart with the gold arrow through it. I asked what the significance was of the arrow and the tattooist said it reflected relationship, romance and a love for someone. You came to mind. I never, ever stopped thinking about you. I never stopped wondering if there was a way in life for me to end up back here with you like this. I wanted to carry the idea of you with me. That's why I got the gold arrow straight through the heart. I didn't think you would ever forgive me, but I never wanted to forget the first man I fell in love with.

Since then, still the only man I've been with. That meant something deep to me."

Carlos kissed the side of her neck, allowing his lips to linger there.

"So much has occurred after you left me. I was lost. Women became a thing."

"Don't. If you're going to fill my head with images of you with a plethora of women, I don't think I can handle that. I didn't know I would be coming back. There is no way I would expect you to think that we'd be like this again. Women are different. I am different. I know who you are. I know what you're like. Every single woman was lucky."

"Still, none were you. I can admit that there were a lot of them. None captured any part of me the way you did from the moment we met."

"Do I still?"

"Baby, I'm still trying to wrap my head around all that happened."

"Do you believe me when I say...?"

"What? That you didn't let Hamilton touch you in any way? Yes, I do believe you. There are some things I trust and don't trust about words that come out of someone's mouth. You lying to me about that would be an even bigger betrayal. I can't see you doing that, so yes, I do believe you. If I thought otherwise, we wouldn't be here. I would be open to helping you, but loving you if I thought he'd done the same is something I wouldn't be able to do. I've shared a lot of things with friends over the years, especially Ham. Though none were women, I do know that there never would be. That's not who I am."

"What will happen when all of this is over? Do we go our separate ways? Stay sex buddies? Other women? I'm sorry if I'm pushing for something that I'm not entitled to."

Carlos knew at this point that he didn't want anyone else. He wasn't sure he was ready to admit that yet.

"I can't say right now what will happen with us when things are over. I'm protective of you. That's something you know. I enjoy being with you. You know that already as well. What do you want?" he asked.

"You. I want you and me. I have no right to ask for that. I want to be honest. I get that there is no picking up where we left off. I don't even know what starting over would look like. Yes, I came to you because I wanted your help. I also came to you because in my life, you have been my one and only safe space. I understand if in your heart you don't trust me fully. I wouldn't either. All I can ask is if you can consider giving me another chance with your heart, I will never give you a reason to regret doing so. I didn't come from love. Until I met you, I didn't know love. I truly thought the decision I made was to protect you. When I found out what my father was capable of, I thought I was thinking of you first the way that you have protected and thought about my safety since I've been back."

"I get that and it's okay. Let's get through all of this and see where it goes. If we're meant to be together again, nothing will be able to come between us. We both know what that's like. We have to choose to never want to be in that place again. Tonight, all I want to do is love you. The world around us is crazy. I have a few hours before I need to get to work. I have a lot of meetings over the next few days. You have several meetings and court dry-runs with your attorney. I want us both to focus on those things. I don't want you to worry about whether I want you or not. I do. I questioned myself about that, but I am certain that my heart remembers you. My body thrives for you. My soul is invested in you."

Before he could continue, Everly shifted and the bubbly water sloshed around them. She turned and straddled his lap so that they were facing each other, her legs on either side of his.

"All of me thrives for you. I know what it's like to not have you and I don't want to go back to that. I am happy where we are right now. I know it's new and it happened fast just like the first time we met. You, Mr. Kincaid, are the only man that I've ever had sex with on the first date. I can't say I've had to sex life that you have, but my usually time frame is often months. There was something about you that night. That feeling never left me. Neither has this feeling."

Carlos didn't know what she meant by this until her hand slipped below the water and grasped him tight, gliding her hand up and down him. The unexpected act not only surprised him, but reminded him of how good they still were together. That night on the car at a placed they used to love going to in order to tune out the world was his first reminder that perfection came in the form of Everly Robinson. When she used both of her hands, her eyes connecting with his on a deeper level, he held his breath through the exhilarating feeling her touch brought to his body. He kissed her. As her hands moved up and down his flesh, he took her mouth, nibbling on her lips before going in for a much more intimate encounter. She tasted like strawberries, no doubt as a result of the wine glass he saw on the ledge at the foot of the tub. He moved her hair before placing his hands on either side of her face before kissing her deeper, showing her how he couldn't wait to make love to her body the same, sensual, amorous way. He pulled her close, pressing his solid body against her soft breasts. He could feel how fast and damn near erratically fast her heart was beating through her chest.

Her hands continued to stroke him and he worked to calm his raging hardness. He wanted to wait to release his love inside of her body. Her hands were burning through the little shred of resistance he had about their next step. He thought that topic was over for now, but his body was screaming he wanted her and only her from this point forward.

"You're killing me," he uttered into her mouth after pulling out and going back in again.

His hands moved down to stroke and caress her breasts which were full and heavy in his hands. Her body writhed wildly on his lap. Her hands felt so good stroking and cupping him that he needed to stop before he got to where he wanted to be; inside of her.

Moving her hands away, he smiled against her mouth when she grunted her displeasure that he wouldn't allow her to continue. He quickly slipped his hand between her opened legs and wasted no time in distracting her with his fingers stroking her this time. He played in her wetness, moist for more than just being in water. The slippery feeling told him that she was as aroused and ready as he wanted her to be. He still wanted a little more before he slid inside of her.

Slipping first one, then two fingers inside of her, he nipped at her neck while his free hand tweaked her nipple into a hardened pebbled that was screaming for his tongue.

When Everly reached out and grabbed his shoulders, leaning her head back, hips grinding against his hand, he knew the multiple points that he was stimulating would send her over the top. He loved watching her face in the throes of a powerful release. He was about to watch another.

"Are you going to come for me, baby. You know I love to watch you at that ep."

Carlos stroked her pointed clitoris with his thumb as his index and middle fingers continued to plunge into depth of her waiting body. She set the rhythm, pumping up and down on his fingers, going faster and fast.

"Son of a bitch!" she yelled.

Carlos grinned knowing what was next. Her mouth and her body screamed at the same time as her fingernails dug into his shoulder. The feeling of pain and pleasure that stirred in him was well worth the visual in front of him as Everly let go and throbbed and clenched around his fingers. He had to move his hand down to the small of her back to hold onto her body as she thrashed about, clenching her bottom lip between her teeth.

"Yes, baby! My, my you are so beautiful when you give into the feeling by letting it take over you."

Everly moaned as her hips slowed to a slight grind, eyes closed as she rode out the vestiges of her shattering release. He wanted to give her more; much more.

Before her body calmed too much, he gripped her behind, lifting her up and over top of his strained hardness. He guided her into a slow glide down on him until the hitch in her breath told him that he was fully seated inside of her. When her inner walls tightened around him, he braced them with his elbows on the edge of the tub because his hands were busy gripping her breasts, pulling them close together to allow his mouth easy access to go swiftly between the two nipples. Everly screaming his name, encouraging her by her lips rocking back and forth, her eyes staying on his. They enjoyed watching each other love on each other.

His hips thrust up deep into her in a slow grinding motion. There were times when he enjoyed surging inside of her with hard, powerful strokes, but right now wasn't the time for time. He wanted to love her slowly. He wanted them to focus on the motion of their hips as they loved in a temporary world where only the two of them existed. He could be happy being inside of her forever. The idea sent a fire through his body when he answered her question about if he could see them together again beyond these moments. His body and mind were now in sync. He knew the answer was yes. His mouth was hungry for every part of her. His mouth lingered over every part of flesh he could get contact with. The slow grind had to come to an end as her body deliciously possessed him; his own release was mere seconds away. The way Everly was moving ferociously on top of him, she was close as well. He wanted them reaching the ultimate precipice together.

Carlos moved his hips faster, his entry in and out of her body quickened. Everly placed her hands on his chest to brace herself and he knew what was next. She rode him. She rode him hard and fast; they moaned loudly together.

"Yes, baby. Give me all of you. Together with me," Carlos crooned into her neck. As one, they ascended to the peak of desire and soared to higher heights, shedding all inhibitions as they surrendered to each other, dazzling quivers rocking their bodies into a blissful haze of carnal eroticism. They stayed that way for what seemed an eternity. He held her close and her pliant body splayed out across his. Then something hit him. This wasn't the time to think of another man but an untruth struck him, slamming into him like a brick building collapsing all around him. Everly moved out of his embrace and looked at him quizzically.

"Your body suddenly stiffened and not in the way that I love. What happened?" she asked.

He hesitated knowing the timing sucked. He had to ask.

"Nathaniel Briggs."

"Ham's father?"

"Yes. He lied to me earlier. I don't think he came here because he thought you were here. He knew. He was too confident that you would come to me. He was too sure that I knew where you were. How? How did he know?"

Everly didn't look away in shame. He was happy for that. There was only one way Nathaniel would come knowing he would get the help he needed. He was already so self-assured in his plan.

"My attorney told him. She leaked information to him that I was here in hopes that he would tell Hamilton. My team needed him to come out of hiding. She assumed he would do so for his father. Carlos, I promise, I wasn't keeping anything from you. I wasn't. She was trying to take the heat and work off of you. I didn't want you to get too involved. I don't think she believed he would come here. Her assumption was that Hamilton would show up."

When Everly looked like she would cry, he put his finger to her lips to silence her.

"Baby, it's okay. I promise you, I'm not mad. I was also surprised that he would show up. The fact that your attorney had a plan to get Ham out of hiding was brilliant. He was lurking to the point that we couldn't find him. He will come out for his father if he thought he would help him. In a way, this is helping Ham. It's also going to help you and that's all that matters. I'll take any leak as long as we can get to the end of all of this and find a way to get you your freedom back."

Everly's eyes dropped.

"You're not upset with me for not telling you?"

"Baby, you need to keep what happens between you and your attorney between the two of you. She is the best and she knows what is best for you. That is all that matters. We're good. Okay?"

Everly kissed him and nodded. Even though he assured her they were okay, she still cried. He kissed her tears away.

"Okay. The water has gotten cold. We should get out before we both end up with wrinkly skin."

"Hungry? I have a few hours before work."

"I'm starved. Working up an appetite with you is a given. I'll order something good unless you have a taste for something."

Carlos looked her up and down before winking with a raunchy, lust-filled look on his face.

"You don't want to know."

"Oh, I can feel, so I already know. Let's eat and then..."

"I can eat?" he interrupted and asked.

"You have to make it dirty. I love it. Yes, and then you can eat yet again."

~ ~

Hamilton ended the call with his father. Even though he had embarrassed him to the entire world, he was still willing to help him.

"Your father found her?" the man in the back seat asked him.

Hamilton turned his head and looked at him before turning to the driver of the black Navigator truck. They had been riding around for over an hour checking the few places he thought Carlos may help with stashing Everly if she did, in fact, come to him when she returned to Chicago. Where else would she go? She didn't have anyone else. She had one other friend, but finding her was harder than it had been to find Cecily. The way his men had beat her he wasn't expecting. That also told him that Arlo wasn't playing around. He wanted the heat off of them and Everly was the key to get that done.

"He didn't say that exactly. He only said he has a plan to get to her. He's got the money and the means to do it. The heat will come off of him too if Everly disappears. It's a win-win all around."

"He had better be okay with the plans we have for her. You had better be too. Arlo has a pot of gold for us if we can pull this off. He wants her gone. You're good with that too, right?"

"Absolutely. She was a prude anyway. She wouldn't let me have a little taste. I once heard her with Carlos and she seemed like she'd be a lot of fun."

"Well, maybe we'll let you have a little fun before we kill her."

Hamilton shook his head from side to side. He had no interest in an unwilling woman.

"Nah, I'm good. My interest in her waned a long time ago. I want this over with so that I can head of into the sunset and spend my money that Arlo is holding onto. A few more days and this will be over."

"Bet," the driver said.

Hamilton sneered. He was ready to be done with them too. Being babysat wasn't his idea of a pleasantry. His father would never forgive him with his latest lies but he didn't care. He never liked the man anyway.

15

"Horace. I need your truth here. How much are you missing Las Vegas?"

Horace Grant looked across the card table, his eyes focused on Torrence's card dealing and not the facetious look he knew he would see. He'd been in Chicago a short time to oversee the construction of the new casino while also having Torrence's back as he stepped back from running their first Chicago casino. His plan was to stay a few months and then head back to the Las Vegas casino they owned together. Right now, a few months looked like it was going to be more than just a few. He picked up his cards for the three-hand game of poker that he, Torrence and Carlos were playing, pausing before he answered. They were in the lower-level area of Torrence and his wife, Reese's Chicago home; the space he called his man-cave.

"I think his silence means he does, considering the last walkthrough of the property I did with him yesterday didn't give him the results he had hoped for," Carlos said.

Torrence stopped dealing. Horace lowered his head. He knew the events of the day before would come up.

"What? Something isn't on schedule? You promised to keep me up to date if I didn't show up to hover over the inspection," Torrence noted.

"I know, I know. I didn't feel like the stress of it all today. We agreed to get together for some cards, beers and no work talk," Horace said.

"I get that, but still, if something is going on that I need to weigh in on, don't keep it from me. I appreciate you giving up your life in Vegas to help me with the casinos in Chicago. Now, with Reese and this difficult pregnancy now my priority, it feels criminal to leave you to handle it all."

"Torrence, I'm not handling it all by myself. We have an entire team of developers, planners, construction, architecture, etc, along with security which Carlos here is overseeing. You know how expertly his teams does their job."

"Yeah, I have his back. That's why I did the walkthrough of not just the casino but the property with him yesterday. Don't worry about anything," Carlos said to Torrence.

"That's easier said than done. Our doctors keep telling Reese and I not to worry about the baby, but you know what, I worry anyway."

"Is anything wrong that makes you concerned?" Horace asked. "That's why I came so that all you would need to focus on was her and your baby."

"No, she's actually doing a lot better than she was a month ago. We had a scare when she started spotting. Her doctor still suggested she stay off of her feet as much as possible. She's not on bedrest, since she's clearly not here now. She's at Carter and Sienna's house. Two pregnant ladies just having a good time of being pampered, from what she told me before Sienna picked her up. The baby is doing good at this point. We don't have much longer now though the baby will most likely come a little early."

"Hey, man. Don't worry too much. I'm sure your doctors are all over any issues."

"Speaking of issues. What happened at the construction site?" Torrence asked, turning to Horace and then to Carlos. When Torrence pointed to Carlos to respond, the card game temporarily stopped.

"We have a few kids who tried to break in. They did a little damage but didn't get far because my guys were on top of it. They were playing kid games by tossing firecrackers over the fence into a pile of rock. Horace, do you want to take up the issue with the pond?" Carlos asked.

"It's not a big deal, but I guess it could be. The surveyor found an issue with the pond. Even after it's drained and filled in, there is concern about the foundation under it and how long it would sustain the casino being built over it. We have an additional structural engineer coming in next week with his team to give us another opinion on what they see and think. Overall, construction will be delayed but not stopped all together."

"Man, you've known all of this and I'm just hearing about it," Torrence questioned.

"I promise I have this all covered. I'm not heading back to Vegas anytime soon. I know the plan was for me to return once the foundation was laid but I'm actually enjoying being in Chicago. I've made arrangements that will secure the running of the Las Vegas location for as long as we need. I'm here for the foreseeable future. Look, everything is fine. We said we were getting together to not talk shop and here we are talking shop. I'm glad Reese is better. Carlos, what's the latest with Everly? Are you still ducking and dodging her? Your team has some serious security around her after that first incident. Do you know how she's doing?"

Carlos looked to both men and lowered his head, closing his eyes knowing that these guys were like brothers to him. He could be honest and not be judged. Still, he was judging himself. He was finding each day harder and harder to stay away from Everly and to stay out of her body. The memory of her didn't do justice to his reality of her now being with him.

"She's good. No, I'm not avoiding her anymore. In fact."

He stopped short of blurting it out. Assuming Torrence knew something from Reese didn't appear to be the case. Truth was, he thought that Everly would have let it slip by now that they were spending a lot of time behind closed doors and between the sheets. There was no sign of awareness of Torrence's face.

"Well?" Torrence pushed.

"Everly and I have been spending some time together during my downtime and when she's not meeting with her attorney. Things in the case have taken a turn that has me wrapped up in it. I'm working that out in my head."

"Something dangerous? What do you need from us?" Horace asked.

"It's nothing I can't handle. Hamilton is in town. He's looking for Everly," he explained.

"What? He is actually stupid enough to come back to the scene of the crime? He must be getting help," Torrence said.

"I had a feeling he was back. One of Everly's friends was attacked recently. That leads back to Hamilton and the goons Everly's father employs. They really beat this woman up bad. Put her in the hospital. She's out now. I sent some folks to keep an eye on her and her family. Here's now here and on the hunt."

"Is his father in on helping him stay hidden?" Torrence asked.

"No. He's actually the main person trying to bring him in. I met with him a few days ago. He's leaked the information that Hamilton is back but only to me; not the authorities. He's afraid of what will happen to him if the feds get a hold of Ham's location. His father is behind the new information that was leaked to the feds about the scam. He wants his son to stand up for the crimes he's committed. Ham has hurt so many people, especially Everly. She's doesn't have the cleanest hands in all of this. Clean or soiled, I will kill Hamilton if he even attempts to harm her in any way. Thankfully, his father gets that and he has an idea."

"Do you think Hamilton would go out in a blaze of fire if confronted by the feds? Would he hesitate to do something to you if he's cornered?" Horace inquired.

"I don't know if he's crazy enough to go up against that level of fire power. Everly's father's men though? They would in a heartbeat," Carlos responded.

"I take it Everly doesn't have a relationship of any kind with her father?" Torrence asked.

"She does and it's all bad. They have been estranged for years until he came up with this scheme with Hamilton that drew her in. She never wants to have anything else to do with her father. He'll probably remain free and in hiding in some other country which she doesn't care about. One thing is for sure, we don't get to choose our family," Carlos noted.

"You know if you need us for anything that's coming up, we're a phone call way. As for family, we're definitely that.

We're brothers. The entire group of us. As for Everly, I'm not sure how you're feeling about this but it sounds to me like you're her family. I know how things ended before. There is something different about you when her name comes up," Torrence said.

Carlos didn't try to avoid eye contact this time. He was right, he was Everly's family. He was far from that kind of thinking while she was gone. They've had some amazing days and nights together. He could say it was all about the great sex but it wasn't. She was different. He knows he's different. Everly came back to Chicago a broken woman with the world on her shoulders. She's a woman ready to take whatever punishment comes her way. He was her protector. He wanted to focus on not letting her pay for something that she had good intentions about before she knew the downside.

"She is my family. I'm still in love with her," he admitted.

"You said you've been spending time together. I hope that means you're giving her body a rest; in between," Torrence joked.

"Haha. I know you're not talking. We all know about all the clandestine meetups you and Reese would have; getting it in wherever. I can't lie that being with her again stirred up old feeling. Those old feelings have become good, new feelings. We just have to get beyond all this Hamilton drama. On Friday, his father and I are going to try and talk Hamilton into giving himself up. He thinks his father is siding with him about silencing Everly in order to keep his father's company afloat while also setting Hamilton free because Everly will not be around to tell all that she knows. Little does he know that she has shared enough that he will never be free to roam in a country that has extradition. He's cocky enough to think that getting rid of her will rid him of his problems too."

"You know you have us if you need us to help in any way. I'm wondering if he'll come in willingly. He's got a lot to lose," Torrence said.

"True. I've thought about that too. He's already risking a lot coming back here. He has his heart set on doing something to Everly to keep her quiet. I will never let that happen. The man has become a staunch enemy. I still don't want to see him end up dead. That would kill his parents. I don't think Everly will ever be free if he doesn't turn himself in and tell the truth. He will definitely go to jail but coming in may help with the amount of time he would have to serve especially if he returns the money."

"Do you think he has it to return?" Horace asked.

"I don't know. He's probably got some of it. I'm sure Everly's father has taken a huge chunk of it of which no one will ever see again. I'm just ready for this all to be over with," Carlos admitted.

"So that you and your lady love can move forward into a future together?" Torrence inquired.

Carlos waited and then nodded. That was his plan exactly.

"I'm ready to move forward into a life with her. I didn't think we'd ever be here again, but we are. We've learned so much in the time we were apart. I trust that our bond is stronger. We know what we would lose if we let our love slip through our fingers again."

"Have you told her that?" Horace asked.

"No. I want to clear all of this mess up so that we are free to talk about our future. I don't know what that looks like until she's free from it all."

"What if she goes to jail?" Torrence questioned.

Carlos hadn't thought about that. He still didn't want to think about it though it could be their reality soon.

"I don't know. I can only say that I love her. She is my life. Jail or no jail, I will stand with her. Friday will either be the answer to our prayer or it will leave us with even more questions. We shall see."

As cards were once again being dealt, Carlos allowed his mind to wander to a time in the future when he and Everly could get back to life and love. That was all he could hope for. That was all he wanted.

16

Worry had Everly running on her treadmill like a mad-woman. Tonight was the night that Carlos was set to go with Nathaniel to meet up with Hamilton. A week ago, Carlos made love to her in the tub and then in bed for hours until he went to work, exhausted, she was sure. She surprised herself by sleeping through the night and well into the morning. They didn't get a chance to spend much time together due to work for him and meetings with her attorney for her. Her latest meeting gave her cause for concern. There was a case being built up against her that appeared to be air-tight. The bright spot in it all was that there was a possibility that Hamilton could be brought in. If so, and he could be persuaded to tell the truth, her sentence may not be too harsh. He was the one who got her in this mess. He was also the only person who could help her get out of it.

Before he left for work the night before, he assured her that she had nothing to worry about. He would do everything in his power to convince Hamilton to do the right thing. Carlos couldn't imagine Hamilton living a life on the run. Hamilton played tough. She wasn't sure he was now that the law was looking for him. Her father was behind Hamilton's boldness of the moment. Arlo was the true menace.

When her legs started to burn from the severe workout, she finally turned off the machine and stepped off of it. She leaned over with her hands on her knees until her breaths slowed. Sweat dropped from her forehead to the floor. When her eyes focused on the drops, the world fell away and all she could see was Carlos not coming back to her. What if things went wrong? That was the question she had posed to her lawyer the day before. She had tossed back and forth between telling Nadine what Carlos and Nathaniel had planned. Of course, Nadine's first response was to let the authorities handle things. She wanted Carlos to stay out of it. In the middle of their meeting, Nadine called Carlos on the speaker phone in her office to dissuade him about meeting up with Hamilton. She didn't want him putting his life in danger. Surprising her, Carlos blurted out that there wasn't anything he wouldn't do to help save the life of the woman he loved. He professed his love several times.

Hearing Carlos say again and again how much he loved her brought Everly to tears. She didn't realize he felt that way. Yes, they had gotten close again, but hearing him declaring his love was love for him on another level. Nadine saw her tears and knew her plight. She heard the seriousness in Carlos' voice and knew that she had to let him do what he was going to do. He promised her that he wasn't going into this alone. He had several of his guys standing by. He also reminded her that he was licensed to carry a gun and he was going to have two on him. Not necessarily for use on Hamilton but for anyone with him who thought they were going to try him. After a lot of back and forth, Nadine backed off.

Everly was not going through the waiting game. It had been hours since Carlos last reached out to her by text with a text with nothing but hearts in it. When her cell phone rang, she thought it was him and leaped for it before it stopped. Instead of Carlos, there was a number she didn't recognize. She decided to not answer it. When it stopped ringing, there was the sound of a text message. She checked and no, it wasn't Carlos. She was still excited beyond belief. There was a text from Cecily saying it's her that's calling. Everly dialed the number right back.

"Cecily?" she asked when the phone was answered on the first ring.

"It's me."

They both began to cry profusely. Neither was able to speak. When she could finally find her words, Everly spoke up first.

"I'm so sorry. I am so, so sorry about what happened to you. Everything is my fault. I've been so stupid and naïve. Are you okay?" Everly asked in a pleading voice.

"It's okay. I'm fine. You could not have known something like this would have happened. I promise you, it's okay. If it wasn't, I wouldn't be calling you. Carlos' friend gave me this number before he left the other day. He said when I was ready that it would be safe to call you. Are you okay?"

Everly nodded and wiped her tears away forgetting she wasn't on video.

"I'm fine. Carlos is taking great care of me. He's been protecting me."

"I'm glad that's where you went when you came back. Melvin said you had come here first looking for me. I was out of town until the day I was attacked. I had just come home and some men followed me into my building. I was oblivious to who they were. I didn't sense any danger. When I opened my door, they rushed in. I still can't remember anything. A neighbor called the police."

"Oh, I'm sorry. How are you coming along? I wish I could see you to give you a hug and apologize."

"Don't you dare apologize again. I will heal. I have also learned to watch my surroundings better. Anyway, enough about the bad parts of what has happened. I'm happy that you're back. Most of all, I'm happy you returned to Carlos. He really missed you. He was angry at the world but Nola and I checked up on him. We knew something had to happen that was untoward that pulled you away. I kept saying it had to be something else. You were never attracted to that man. He was good looking, but he was handsome slime."

Everly wanted to cry more. Cecily hit it on the head with where her own head has been. She still can't figure out how she couldn't think to make a different choice other than following Hamilton and her father and not the man who loved her.

"I want to explain everything to you," she offered.

"No, sis. Let me set something straight right now. All that is over with. I know what you're going through now. I'm thankful that you're healthy and in your right mind. I believe you will survive this. As soon as I am healthy enough, I'll be in Chicago to visit and support you. I don't need the back story. I'm just happy that you're back. Are you still with Carlos? His friend said you were staying with him."

Everly smiled remembering where she and Carlos were now. Nothing would ever take her away from him again.

"Well, I'm not staying with him, with him, but I am where he is. I can admit that we've been together, together, if you know what I mean. And, it's been amazing. I forgot how attentive he is. I appreciate him more than I ever have. So much about his I took for granted. There is so much I need to bring you up to date on. Even right now, he's out trying one last ditch effort to save me. I will never be able to thank him enough."

"I'm sure he doesn't expect a thank you. He wants your love. He needs your love. You need him. I'm glad you found your way back to each other. Whatever he's out doing, he'll be successful because I believe he wants the chance to love you again without all of this hanging over your relationship. Carlos can take care of himself."

"You're right. I wish I had known that back when I left. I should have trusted that he can handle anything that comes his way. I've been anxious all evening knowing that he's putting himself in danger because he's fighting for my freedom."

"Let me help you stay further distracted until he comes back to you. Tell me what it's like being back in the arms of the man you love."

Everly moved to the bed and laid across it. She had a lot to tell Cecily. She was right. Her eyes were going to stay on the door until Carlos returned. She trusted he would be safe.

~~

"Boss, if anything jumps off, you know I've got your back. What do you see from where you are?" Melvin questioned.

Carlos looked around at the darkened pier where Nathaniel stood on the edge near the water. It was where he told Hamilton he would meet him. The location was on property owned by a friend of Nathaniel. He had arrived before Nathaniel so that he and his men could search the area. Thankfully, they didn't encounter anything or anyone that gave them pause. They were only a few minutes from the time Hamilton said he would be here.

"My eyes are on Nathaniel. Once I set my eyes on Hamilton, I'll get out of the car."

"Sounds good. I'll be close by. You may not see me but know that I'm right there with you."

"Brother, I have no doubt. I've seen you operate in stealth mode. I feel sorry for anyone who decides to test you tonight. I'm good on my end. You know I'm strapped. Hey, I see him. I see Ham. He just walked up to his father."

"I just got a text from one of my men. He just noted that Hamilton was walking up. Stay alert, Boss. I got you."

Carlos disconnected the call and stepped out of the car. He could hear Hamilton and his father talking about Everly. Whatever was said didn't sit well with Hamilton. He didn't want to delay their interaction too long. This face-to-face had been put off for far too long.

The minute he left the shadow of the tall factory building, Hamilton was the first to see him. Carlos noted that for a split second, Hamilton had decided to make a run for it when he realized it wasn't Everly but him that showed up. Then the man stopped. Carlos didn't walk right up to them. He left some distance between them.

"Oh, so what is this? Did you bring the feds with you? The prince of all things good and clean," Hamilton declared facetiously.

"Not happy to see me? Expecting someone else, Ham?" Carlos shot back at him. He was dressed in all black, including a black bomber jacket that hid both guns on either hip.

"Pop, what's this?" Hamilton asked his father.

Carlos watched his eyes dart in all directions. Most likely, he was expecting the feds to come from the shadows as well. He knew they were looking for him.

"Son, I asked Carlos to come. Listen, how you've been going about this isn't the way. I can't let you hurt anyone else. I asked Carlos to come to help me talk you into coming in unharmed. This has gone on long enough," Nathaniel explained.

"Ham, you knew your father wasn't going to bring Everly here to you. Aren't you tired of running? Can you see yourself living on the run for the rest of your life? That's what will happen. The longer you stay connected to her father, the worse things will be for you," Carlos explained.

"So, she's with you, huh? She came back to you. I knew it. I've been everywhere trying to find how she's moving about to and from the courthouse without any trace. I said to myself that it had to be you. Who else would go to such lengths to keep her safe. You. Only you, the infamous Carlos."

"Ham, I'm not the infamous one. That would be you. I'm here to help because your father asked me to."

"Oh? How's Everly? She's definitely smarter than I thought she was. Her leaving and coming here could destroy me and her. She didn't get that. She came back to her precious Carlos thinking you can save her. You didn't save her the first time and you won't this time. You have no idea what her father is capable of. If I don't take care of this, he will find me. He will find her. You can't protect her forever."

Carlos laughed. Even now, Hamilton was still trying to be a big shot. He allowed him to catch him slipping once, but never again. He was leaving with Hamilton by any means necessary. That was the only way to get some of the weight of the scam off of Everly's back. Now that he has her back, he would give up everything to keep her on the outside of a jail cell.

"Ham, I'm not sure how you got back in this country. You have to know you can't get back out. Every way of that could be possible transportation for you is on the lookout for you."

Hamilton laughed.

"They have no clue I'm in this country. If they did, I'd already be in handcuffs. The only people who know are you and my father."

"And every federal agency that I could contact," Carlos admitted.

He may be desperate to save his woman, but he's not stupid enough to do it on his own.

"Carlos?" Nathaniel questioned. "We had a deal," he added.

"No, sir. You made a deal with me. I didn't make one with you. The only person who matters to me is Everly. I don't give a damn about Ham or you, for that matter. Ham has to come in and deal with this. Ham, you know this was wrong. You know that this will never be over even if Everly goes to jail. Her father is still out there. A man like that will never let you be free. Everly will talk; that's a given. She will be protected. That's also a given. You can be protected but only if you come in. No one else needs to be hurt; not like Cecily. No more, Ham. Enough is enough. Is that who you are now? You beat up innocent women? Who the hell are you?"

When Ham walked toward him, Carlos moved his jacket to the side and made sure he saw the weapon there. Hamilton quickly put his hands in the air in the surrender stance.

"You going to shoot me? Is that where we are now? All this for a woman I stole from you?"

"You didn't steal her from me. You threatened the lives of the people she loved the most. She was vulnerable and you took advantage of that."

"How much you will never know," Hamilton said and laughed.

"I would dignify that with anger but there is no need. You may have preyed on her but anything else is all in your mind, bro. Don't even go there. If I thought that were true, I would take my chance in jail and fill you full of holes. As it stands, you're not worth the effort or the jail time; not for me and not for Everly. The only chance you will ever have of staying alive is to come in. Did you know that Arlo put a price, not only on her head, but yours too? You didn't wonder where the two men who have been following you around like a second skin are?"

"What are you talking about?"

"The feds got a wire that Arlo put a price on your head after you took care of his daughter. Are you insane? This is the person you decide to get in bed with? He leaked information about you to those two guys. You were going to be a dead man if Everly had shown up tonight. The two of you would have shared the same grave. You thought they let you come alone tonight? That call made to you about the rendezvous spot once you had Everly with you was a ploy. They're in custody and under arrest for attacking Everly's friend in New York. A neighbor recognized them. A lot has happened today while you were out trying to scope out where Everly was."

"You are turning me in? All because I took your woman? You're that whipped?" Hamilton laughed again.

"Go with whatever you want to call it. At this point, I don't care. She's here in Chicago and she's safe. No one will be able to touch her. The feds are willing to make a deal with you. They want the money back. They also want Arlo. His men are singing like canaries. If they are able to share a tip on where Arlo is and he's captured before you can take the same deal, they'll come out on top. You'll still be out here trying to hide in more shadows. Come in and let your father help you get through this."

"Ham, listen to him. There is no other way out of this. Thanks to Carlos, he was able to work out a deal if he could bring you in. He's got connections that allowed him to do this for me. I don't want to bury my only son. I know we haven't had the best relationship, but I'm here for you now. Please let us help you."

When Hamilton reached for something in his pocket, Carlos removed the safety and drew his gun. To his left, beyond where Ham and his father stood, he saw Melvin, like him, dressed in all black from head to toe.

"Whoa! I don't have a gun; no weapon at all," Hamilton said.

Carlos watched his eyes dart around as other men came from the shadows. They were all his men.

"Ham, just come with me. This needs to come to an end. I can't leave here without you. You have destroyed enough lives. You have a chance to save Everly's. I know you don't care much about that because of me. I get that. She's innocent in this and you know it. Don't make her pay because she has the world's lousiest father. She deserves better than prison."

"What? She deserves better? She deserves you, I guess you're trying to say."

"She does. Besides that, she deserves as much freedom as she can get. She can only get that if you come in and help the feds get back what's not yours or Arlo's. You have a shot at a good deal. Jail time is in your future. Not as much as it would be if you don't come in right now and deal with this. You don't deserve my help, but I'm offering it to you. If you try to run, you won't make it far. Do the right thing."

"Ham, please. I'm begging you to listen to Carlos. No more running," Nathaniel said.

"Ham? Ham? Is that you?"

Carlos turned to Nathaniel who held up his phone in speaker mode. On the other end was his wife.

"Ma?" Ham questioned.

"Yes. It's me. Please don't do this. It's been a year. I've missed you. Your father and I are here to help you in any way we can. You have to come in and answer for what you've done. I'm begging you. Let Carlos take you in. He didn't have to help you. Those men were going to kill you. You're not safe out in the street. Enough is enough."

For the first time in his life, Carlos saw a vulnerable part of Hamilton. The man's shoulders slouched as his head dropped down. He may have been on the outs with his father over the years, but he loved his mother. Calling her had been his idea. Nathaniel wasn't for it at first. Carlos knew that if Hamilton could hear his mother's voice, that was all that would be needed to reach the reasonable side of him.

"Ma, you don't understand," Hamilton declared softly.

He was close, Carlos thought.

"Come in and talk to me about it. Live another day and then another day. I will be here for you always. You have to make this right. That young woman doesn't deserve to take the hot seat for something you put into play. Let us help you. Please!"

Carlos waited. He put his gun back on his hip and waved Melvin and his other men off.

"Ham, what's it gonna be? Your mother is right. Everly doesn't deserve this. You've hurt her enough. It's time to stand up and be a man," Carlos said.

Again, he waited.

In a move that surprised them all, Hamilton put his hands up in surrender and then placed them behind his back as if he were waiting for handcuffs.

"I'm sorry, Pop," Hamilton said.

Carlos waited when Hamilton's eyes locked with his.

"I'm sorry Car. There was a time when I considered you a friend. I'm sorry I hurt you. I'm especially sorry for what I took Everly through. I will say that for an entire year, she never stopped declaring how much she loved you. I hated that but I respected it. I'm ready."

Carlos nodded without acknowledging the apology. He wasn't ready for that just yet. He took out his phone and pressed one number. When he did, a few seconds later, a black sedan sped up. Out of it jumped three men. Everything after that happened fast. Hamilton was walked to the back of the car and placed in the back seat. When the car pulled away, he turned to Nathaniel.

"I'm sorry, sir. I know this wasn't the exact plan we talked about."

"Son, no worries at all. This is better than having to see my son on a medical examiner's table. I will take this any day over what could have been. Go on back to your lady. Tell her that my family is sorry. I hope Hamilton can make her whole.

She deserves that. She deserves a man like you who would do anything in his power to fix her life and take care of her."

"Thank you, sir. If you need anything else from me, you know how to reach me. I meant what I said to Ham. He's done some dirty things but I am here if he needs me. I don't want to hold a grudge. I want to get back to life with my woman. You're good from here?"

"I'm better than good."

Carlos turned and walked back into the shadows where his car was parked. Looking around to check his surroundings, it didn't escape him that Melvin and his men were gone. They had slipped away as fast as they had come out of the shadows. He smiled knowing that's why he hired them. This is why they were at the top of their game.

Getting in the car, he drove off the pier and raced back to the casino. He would do one quick check and then spend the rest of the night with Everly wrapped tightly around him. He was never letting her go again. It was time to turn the page and start a new chapter. He was more than ready for that.

17

Four Months Later

Everly was too excited to nap like Carlos was doing. They'd had an exciting day with his nephews and her baby sister. All of them were currently laid out across the large sectional in Carlos' spare bedroom at the hotel. She and Carlos were temporarily living together in his suite until the house they were under contract to buy was ready for them to move into after closing took place in two weeks. Things had moved pretty fast for them after Carlos convinced Hamilton to turn himself in. Since that night when Carlos came back to her, they have been inseparable. She was back where she's always wanted to be; with the man who helped her feel complete.

She looked over at Carlos who had his nephews on each of his shoulders; all three of them hit her with soft snores. The home-like feeling gave her delight. She found it adorable.

In her own arms, was her sister, Ariel. Never in her life did she ever imagine she could love someone as much as she loved this four-year-old. She was still in complete shock that Ariel was even with her in the United States. Having her had been the largest part of the turn to how wonderful her life was going compared to how it had started.

After Carlos and Nathaniel had successfully brought Carlos to the feds, both kept to their word that they would give him their support as he went through this tough time in his life. Hamilton had been tried and convicted of too many counts for her to imagine. He'd been given a sentence of forty years in federal prison for his crimes. After all that had occurred, Carlos had stayed in contact with Hamilton. He'd even gone to visit him a few times. Thankfully, Hamilton was getting the mental help that he needed. It's too bad he hadn't gotten that kind of help before everything went to hell in his life.

As for her sister, it turns out that Fancy had in fact been found dead. A woman she'd left Ariel with had reached out to her and told her that her sister was okay. Carlos reached out to some special forces guys he knew out in California who offered to help them get Ariel out of South America. One of the men, Calvin Lymon, had himself gone through something similar when he needed to get his own son out of the same region. Ariel was safely smuggled into the United States and has been with her and Carlos since she arrived. Ariel still misses her mother but has settled in nicely with them. She and Carlos secured an immigration attorney who was helping them secure papers for Ariel to remain with them. They were already thinking with the mindset that they were a family. She couldn't wait to decorate Ariel's room in their new house.

As for her brother Dante, his case was eventually overturned once they were able to get him much better lawyers. It turns out that nothing could be tied directly to Dante other than him being there when everything went down. The women who were a part of the smuggling ring didn't know him and couldn't point him out as someone they had seen helping smugglers transport them. As for the drugs, none were actually found on Dante. Rather, he was there where the drugs were. No link could be made. His lawyers were able to make a good case for his release after the torture from his childhood had been revealed. He was given leniency with the promise that he would go through drug treatment. Carlos had seen to that. He'd worked hard to help Dante get enrolled in a six-month program. Carlos invited Dante to Chicago to stay with them until he got back up on his feet. All he had to do was complete the program. That gave her brother something to look forward to. Besides that, there were a bunch of men, all friends of Carlos, who volunteered to be big brothers to Dante in order to keep him on a path to success.

Looking around at her family, this was the life she had dreamed of. She would never take it for granted again.

Carlos shifted on the chair and then stilled when he remembered his nephews were still asleep on him. He mouthed to her that he needed a way to get them from his arms and into their beds he'd set up in his spare bedroom. He loved being on uncle duty. Alyssa and Dexter were on a weekend getaway and his mother, who usually watched the boys, was herself on a girl's trip with friends. Marlow was away accompanying Joey at a wrestling match in Las Vegas. Not that he considered himself the least of them when it came to looking after his nephews, he was usually so busy that his sister rarely asked him to watch them. With Ariel around, she was someone the boys could play with. This time around when Alyssa and Dex wanted a getaway, Carlos volunteered to host them and even took five days off from work to do so. Everly loved how the boys looked at him like he was a king. He loved them as much as they loved him. He was like a kid with them earlier when they spent the day out.

After taking them to the park, one of their favorite places, they'd gone out for burgers and fries. Once they were back at his place, they had tired themselves out running around chasing each other. When they finally crawled up on him on the sofa, within minutes, they were asleep. Ariel had done the same with her after a full day. They were now faced with putting the kids to bed without waking them. Carlos stood first, moving as not to wake the boys.

Turning to face her, he held up a finger to let her know he'd be right back. She blew him a kiss and waited before standing slowly herself with Ariel in her arms. Once Carlos got them settled, he came back out and took Ariel from her arms so that he could put her down as well.

She began putting away the tons of toys that covered every open space. Carlos smiled at her when he found her in her element. She loved playing mommy to Ariel.

"You don't have to do that," he said, walking over to help her.

"This place looks like a truck backed up to it and dumped a load of toys all over the room. Where did you get all of these? Don't tell me your sister brought these from her house," she laughed.

"I bought all of them. I took note of some of the things she and Dexter had at their house, which actually does look like a toy store. I like that when they come here, they feel at home."

"A week ago and I didn't see any remnants of this many toys."

"They were still packed up in the other bedroom. I always keep some things here for them. We now have to do that for Ariel too. She's with us all the time, so we're used to her stuff. This is the first time the boys are here for a few days."

"You can't blame me for all of these toys that are Ariel's. Thank Sienna, Reese and Marlow for these. Since Reese and Sienna just had babies, they keep sending all of these Amazon boxes filled with clothes and toys for her. Once we move into the house, we will have our own brand of a toy store. I think you love this more than I do. Ariel has renewed my hope in having a full life. She keeps me busy. She keeps you busy too. I love this side of you," she said.

After loading up the two large toy boxes that sat under the wall of windows, they collapsed together on the sofa.

Winking, he leaned close to Everly's face and whispered, "before we say another word, lips please."

The minute they were connected as one, he coaxed her lips open, tasting the sweet nectar of the love the resonated from every part of her. He loved that it was all for him. When her hand lightly touched his face, caressing it as he deepened their sensual connection he gave in to the love that grew day by day between them. Where he was tired after spending the day with three rambunctious toddlers, he was suddenly rejuvenated like a man who was ready to leap a building in a single bound. His proof was the desire for Everly that grew between his legs with a vengeance. He smiled against her lips when her other hand reached down to caress his surging flesh. They were more in sync than ever.

"Only a kiss?" she asked seductively after ending their kiss that they knew would lead to other things.

"Well, that's how it started."

"Mmm, and now we're here," Everly suggestively looked down to where her hand rested.

"You do amazing things to every part of me; sometimes with just a thought of you."

She kissed him quickly one last time and moved her hand. Hitting her with his sad face, she laughed out loud before covering her mouth. He knew she was remembering the kids were asleep.

"We do amazing things to each other. Busy day?"

"Extremely, especially after I got a little work done. Entertaining toddlers is no joke. It's harder than managing a staff of a hundred. I don't see how my sister and brother-in-law keep up with those tow. They do not believe in sitting still unless they're ready for a nap. Can you believe Alyssa wants another baby?"

"Now? Two kids under five and she's ready for a third? That's the sign of a superwoman. Does chasing those two around mean you're exhausted; besides, you know, the obvious?"

Carlos followed her eyes to his lap.

"I'm never, ever too tired for that; not when it comes to you," he quipped. "We'll try and get some alone time in once we know everyone is down for the entire night. I'm glad we fed them early and got baths in early. Alyssa said both boys always sleep through the night. We already know that Ariel does. Sure, it was rough when she first got here a month ago. She really loves you. I guess the two of you bonded in South America."

"Yes, we did. I spent a lot of time with her. She was still trying to understand that I was her sister. As soon as she saw me, she would run to me. A few times, she spent the night with me. She was my comfort while I was there. It's wonderful having her here with us. Fancy wanted this. I think she knew that she wasn't going to get far. The woman who had Ariel said that on the first day that Fancy arrived at her place with Ariel, she felt like she was being followed. She feared for Ariel's life. That's why she left her behind. If they were going to be found, it would be her alone, without Ariel. She didn't want my father to get his hands on her and poison who she could be. I will forever look after her as Fancy would have wanted."

"Fancy would be proud."

"Thanks for not hesitating when it came to getting her here to me by any means necessary."

"Baby, I love you. I would go to the end of the earth for you. Your happiness is all that matters to me. Your love is all that matters. There has been enough drama, lies and mess in our lives lately that it feels good to be in this place in our lives; kids and all. I love what we have. We have a second chance. Just like you, I want that more than anything. We'll get it right this time," Carlos noted.

"I'm still amazed that we're here, like this; together. After all I did," she admitted.

Carlos turned to her and pulled her close.

"Baby, you had a major lapse in judgement. It was wrong, but in the end, you made it right. You were able to help get those people their money back. Yes, you've lost your career, but I never really thought that you were that into being a lawyer anyway. I've always thought that you were simply going through the motions because it's what you went to school for."

"I wish I could say you were wrong, but you're not. I started on that path and just went with it. It was a dream, but not a passion."

Thinking about passion, Carlos lifted Everly from her seat next to him until she was straddling his lap. Reaching down, he slid her loose-fitting dress higher up her hips until his hands were able to cup her ample behind. Moving her hair to one side, he kissed her neck which was now exposed for his taking.

"Speaking of passion, what is yours? What can I do to help you find what you're passionate about career-wise? You can do anything you want. No, you can't practice law, but the sky is still the limit."

"I don't know at the moment. I've been thinking of some things. Right now, all I want is you. I don't want to just sit around. I'm not saying that. I want to focus on Ariel, getting our house set up and decorated. I want to be there for my brother. I want to focus on my life with you. I didn't get it right before. I may not have been ready then. I am now. I was close to never being in your arms again. Right after Hamilton turned himself in, Nadine and her team went to work getting the information they needed from him to clear me. I no longer expected the worse. I also didn't think I'd get off with just a fine and the loss of my license to practice law. I failed but never again. I know what I could have lost and I don't ever plan to be in that position again."

"That sounds good to me. From here and for every moment after this, it's me and you. I have you back. I'm never letting go again. All of me is ready for all of you."

Carlos didn't finish his thought. He needed proof that he wasn't alone. Moving his hands slowly up her creamy thighs, he smiled like a cat with his paw caught in the cookie jar the moment Everly almost leapt off of his lap when his finger encountered first her panties and then the moisture behind them. With a quick flick of his finger, he moved beyond the silky barrier and slipped a finger between them and her womanhood. She was just as eager for more as he was.

"I am just as ready for you. Your touch is all I will ever need," she whispered. "I came ready," she uttered.

When she moved his hands to her hips, still under her dress, he knew what she meant. She wanted him to feel.

They were like-minded.

"Damn! You know how much I love your sexy panties. Remind me to make a donation for many, many more just like these."

By those, he meant the kind that were barely there and tied at her hip. That meant in order to get access to what he wanted, he didn't have to lift her up and slide her panties off. All he needed to do was untie them, just as he was doing now. In a second, the silky material fell away and into his hands. Stuffing them in the pocket of his sweat pants to not forget and leave evidence laying around, he lifted his own hips a smidgen and lowered his pants down.

"If I see or hear either of the boys or Ariel..." she started.

"We'll pretend like we're playing. There will be no harm done. We won't scar my nephews or your sister for life."

Before he could utter any more words, Carlos held his breath the minute Everly rose up and slid down on him with ease. She knew what he liked. Nothing turned him on more than a woman who enjoys taking the lead in intimacy. Feeling her body expand around his was amazing. Gripping her hips, he held on as she moved up and down on him, slowly driving him insane.

"I've waited all day for this," Everly said against his lips. Her hands gripped his shoulders.

"Only all day?" Carlos asked while trying to control his breathing.

"Then, now and forever. I love you, baby."

Everly's hips moved faster before he could respond. He could feel her slick walls milking him for everything he had in him. As much as he wanted this to last all night, they were making love out in the open. It wasn't often that they made love in total silence. Everly gripping her lip with her teeth was her way of holding back a scream because of where they were. The feel of her is something he knew he would never tire of. Only she could have him on the edge so quickly after they'd just begun. And here he was. His body was ready to explode all over and inside of her.

Everly's head thrashed about wildly as she rode him. He loved watching her in the throes of an impending, powerfully titillating release.

Reaching between them, he stroked her womanhood, encouraging her to let go.

"I'm right here with you. Come on and come for me, baby," he whispered against her perfectly puckered lips.

That was all Everly needed to hear. When her mouth opened wide, he smothered her scream with his own mouth, pulling much of her love language back to him. He poured the growl of his own release into her mouth as their bodies released at the same time. He moved up and inside her body with powerful strokes, riding her as hard as she was riding him. When he thought she would fall from his lap, he held on tighter, moving inside of her with the determination of a man willing to give the love of his life every part of him freely. Every time he had the chance to be inside of her, he wanted to make up for all the time he spent apart from her. He needed to wipe away the memory of being with other women who never satisfied him the way she did; fully and completely.

They calmed together. With Everly now planted against his chest, he wrapped his arms around her back and held her tight.

"When did you get stars floating around in the air?" she slurred out, sexily.

Carlos laughed. He was seeing them too. Usually, their intimacy lasted much longer than this. Surely, they were meant to be together because the quickie was just as potent as any other time they've been like this.

"I provided them just for you."

He kissed the part of her lips that he could reach.

"I guess you weren't tired."

"I meant it when I said I'm never too tired for you; especially for loving you. I love you. There is nothing I wouldn't do for you. That includes loving you anytime you want or need me to."

"Even giving me the perfect orgasm when I know those boys drained your energy today? One day, you're going to make the perfect husband and father. You would do everything to make them happy, never choosing one over the other. What an amazing woman the mother of your children will need to be."

"You're speaking as if you're talking about some strange woman that's not you. I know things have moved along quickly with the case and all the drama that followed. I plan to slow us down enough to get married and have an entire house full of babies to spoil and chase around. Do you think you're ready for all of that? I'm not letting you out of my life ever again," he murmured lovingly against her cheek.

"Is this you asking me?"

Carlos leaned her away from him and captured her gaze.

"Baby, you deserve a proposal that will be remembered for a lifetime. You won't know when or where. Just know that it will happen. That is a given."

Her smile told him all he needed to know. Thankfully his sister and sister-in-law were already on the job of planning the most amazing proposal he could put on.

"I'm ready for all of that. I've always wanted to be your wife. I may not have gone about it the right way in proving that, but it's the truest thing I've ever said. I know I need to get my life together. I still need to figure out what I'm going to do for a career. You don't want to be married to a woman who just sits around with no direction."

"You know I've got us. I like waking up with you next to me. I enjoy going to sleep at night while I'm still inside of you like right now. You've always loved real estate. You've always loved watching those shows about selling houses and condos. I know how much you love the idea of selling houses. I remember asking you before why you never got into real estate law. It wasn't law that you loved. It was the idea of real estate."

"You remember that? I picked up on that? I would be fantastic at selling properties. I love everything about real estate," Everly said excitedly.

"How can I help you?" he asked.

"What?"

"Tell me what you need from me to help you grasp your passion and run with it. If that's what you want to do, I'm behind you all the way. Whatever you want to do, I'll be your biggest supporter. I want you to be happy. What else would keep a permanent smile on your face?"

"I do want to pursue that. I've been thinking about it for the past few weeks. When we started looking at houses, I felt the draw even then."

"Then do it. You can do anything you want."

"Well, let me see. I'll have a career that I have dreamed about. One day, I'll be marrying the man of my dreams.

"I'm fine with that. Let's focus on what we'll need first."

Everly looked at him questionably. She had an idea.

"Do you think you know what that is? How about, I rank or needs for now and you let me know if you agree."

"Okay, hit me with it."

Everly was feeling giddy inside. She was more excited than he thought he was.

"For starters, that proposal should be first because we're going to need that big backyard sooner rather than later. We should move into our house as a perfect family; name and all."

"Really? I think we only have a few weeks left before we go to settlement. I thought that you would want a lot of time to plan the perfect wedding months after my perfect proposal."

"I would agree with you if the two of us and Ariel wasn't turning into the four of us in about seven months. Because of that, house definitely second after marriage and then career."

Did he hear her right? Did she just say...

"Wait. Back up, back up, baby."

He found her grinning from ear to ear as if she'd just won the lottery. It was true.

"Something puzzling?" she quipped.

"You're pregnant?"

"There is something in the water that feeds your circle because, yes, I'm pregnant; two months to be exact. I found out two days ago when you were on your way back from checking in on Dante."

Carlos' excitement overwhelmed him. He couldn't sit still any longer. Holding her tight, he stood with her still in his arms. He danced happily around the room.

"Are you kidding me? I'm going to be a father? Don't play with me like this, Everly."

"Baby, I wouldn't do that to you. You're going to be a daddy in seven months. I hope you're ready. I know we didn't plan on this."

"Whew, baby. Sometimes the best plans are those that aren't planned at all. Planned or not, I want you, I want this baby and I want our life together. I don't know where to begin because once you mentioned I'm going to be a daddy, nothing else outside of this baby, Ariel and you matter. Thank you for making me this happy."

"No hesitation? I didn't know if this news would make you happy after all we've been through."

"After all we've been through, we're here. It's you and me forever. The past is behind us. We have what's next to look forward to. Wait until everyone hears about this. There's been baby fever all over our circle of friends. My mother is going to be dancing on a cloud. We have a lot to plan for. We're going to have a wonderful life together. I'm going to see to that."

"No more secrets. No lies. No anything that doesn't keep our love standing and strong. I sorry for all of the lost time."

Carlos kissed away anymore apologies. He was ready to leave all that drama behind and focus only on their lust and love.

"I'm living for now and our future. What has happened is done. We have each other. We have our baby, which I am extremely happy about. The world is what we want it to be. I don't care anything about what happened before. That's old and it's done. In fact, I want to go into the bedroom and show you exactly how much I want to wipe the past away."

Without waiting for an answer, Carlos walked with her in his arms to activate the alarm. After stopping briefly at the door to check on the kids who were still sleeping peacefully, he walked them into the bedroom and closed the door behind them. Tonight, nothing else mattered that wasn't about their love.

18

Six Months Later

Horace walked out onto the patio with Marlow's ringing cell phone in his hand.

"Hey. Alyssa said this was ringing like crazy on the kitchen counter. Joey went into the bedroom to change your daughter so she asked me to bring it out here to you. Baby Maia is a cutie just like her momma," he said.

"Thank you. She is our world. She's got Joey wrapped around the finger for sure. He has no problem changing diapers," she joked.

Marlow looked at her phone. The number calling her cell phone was from a blocked caller.

"That's odd. That's the tenth call in a row that's come through as blocked. Maybe they'll call back," she said.

"Must be important."

"True. Thanks for bringing it out. I was so busy relaxing that I didn't realize I'd left it in the house. This is the most relaxation I've had in a week."

"Right. I hear the baby has been sick. I take it she's better?"

"She is anytime she's in her daddy's arms. Maia is definitely a daddy's girl. I tried to take her to change her and she screamed like she was in pain. The minute he picked her up and she grabbed onto his hair, she was suddenly fine. She is yet another female who is all about her daddy's hair! I have become the third wheel. I'm not complaining at all. He loves daddy duty when he's home."

"Are you heading back out on the road with him soon?"

"I was thinking about it. We're not sure of the plan now that we have the baby. So much has changed. Besides, my brother and even my mother love coming to see the baby. I haven't had this close of a relationship with them in a long time. Maia has brought us together. She clings to my brother as much as she clings to Joey."

"No word on Angel yet? Torrence told me about your sister. I hope that was okay."

Still being in Chicago after a year of moving here, Horace was well woven into the life of all these brothers in Chicago and their families. It's been a long time since he's felt like a part of a real family. He hardly ever spoke of his own and no one asked much about them. That was his preference.

"Oh, sure, that's fine. Nothing yet. The last investigator we hired actually thinks she's back in Chicago. Now that everything around Everly is settled, Carlos has really put people in place to search for her. I'm here if she wants to reach out. I'm not going to keep putting energy into someone who doesn't want me to find them. I have a baby girl now who needs and deserves all of my attention. I feel like Angel is a ghost I'm chasing. Every now and then, I get a quick call from her to say she's fine. Before I can ask anything, she hangs up. It's been like that for a year now. I've moved on. The ball is in her court."

"I get that. I had a brother who was once estranged from our family for whatever reason. My one regret was not being in his corner when he finally reached out. My parents thought tough love was the answer and it wasn't. He felt alone. That loneliness led him to take his own life. If I could do any part of my life over again, it would be to stick by him and be there any and every time he reached out instead of thinking being hard on him was the answer. I hope your sister comes around to see how much you love and care about her."

"Thanks for sharing that. I toss between not letting her have me lingering on like this forever and wondering if I've done enough to bring her back around and into the fold with my family. I vowed to answer anytime she called. If and when she wants a relationship, I will be here. I never want her to feel alone when she has family who still loves her despite her past."

Her phone rang before the conversation could continue. It was the same blocked number. This time she was able to answer.

"Hello?"

"Marlow?

She stood faster than she had planned and almost tripped before Horace was able to catch her.

"Whoa," he said.

"Angel?" Marlow yelled.

People began gathering around her.

"Yes. It's me. I'm in trouble. I'm desperate."

Marlow exhaled. What she didn't want to hear was that Angel was again in trouble because of drugs. She promised herself to not judge but to be what and who Angel needed.

"What kind of trouble?" she asked.

"I'll get Joey," Horace said to the group.

"I've been arrested. I promise, I'm innocent."

"Of what? What are you being accused of?"

"Solicitation. Well, actually, prostitution. I promise you it's not true. I've done some things, but never that."

"Oh, Angel. What have you done? Where are you?"

"Here in Chicago on the west side."

"Okay, I'll be right there."

"No, Marlow. I need you to get my baby. They're putting her in the system. I haven't seen her in a few days. She was with a friend and then this happened. I can't explain it all right now. I need you to go get my baby."

"Baby? You have a baby?"

"Yes. Her name is Marleigh. They won't tell me where she is or what they'd done with her. Please help me."

Stunned, Marlow turned to Joey as he walked up with Maia bouncing in his arms.

"What's going on?" he asked as Alyssa walked over and took the baby out of his arms.

"It's my sister. She's in jail charged with prostitution. She has a baby that's been taken away from her. We have to find the baby and help Angel."

"My attorney's sister is also a lawyer. She specializes in family law. I'll give her a call," Horace said, stepping away while he pulled out his phone.

"We're on our way. Angel, don't worry. I've got you. Where are you?"

After repeating the information as Joey noted it in his phone, she ended the call.

"I've got the baby; go," Alyssa said.

Marlow didn't know what direction to go in after ending the call. Thankfully, Joey did. He took her by the hand.

Marlow stopped and turned to Alyssa before they got too far. Her mind was fried. It was all over the place. First and foremost, there was Maia.

"Everything she needs is in her bag. There is extra milk in Everly's refrigerator," Marlow explained haphazardly.

"I got you covered," Alyssa said.

She then turned to Everly.

"I'm so sorry for interrupting your housewarming party. Issues seem to follow this group around. I guess it's our turn," she said.

She was worried. Her mind was going in a million directions hearing that not only was Angel really in Chicago, but she also had a baby. A *baby?* She had to get to her. Most of all, she needed to find her niece. This was her second chance to help Angel and get it right.

"Baby, they got it. Let's go," Joey said.

"I'm coming with," Horace exclaimed. "I talked with my attorney, Manny and he's reaching out to his sister right now. He'll have her meet us at the jail."

"Thanks for helping, Horace. You don't have to take up your time to go with us," Marlow said.

"Let me help. We were just talking about not taking a gamble when family is in need. Your sister needs you. I want to be of help in any way I can. I'll drive."

Racing to his car, Horace thought back on a time when he wished he'd followed his own instinct instead of listening to his family. He could have helped his brother who was in need. Because of what happened, he had moved away from New York years ago to get away from his family. He chose to move to Las Vegas to start a life that was laced with guilt every day of his life. He didn't want to see his new friends, Joey and

Marlow go through that. He didn't know Angel but she was someone in need. Maybe he could redeem himself for not being able to save his brother when he could. He was ready for a life where he could be of help and not hide behind being a busy casino owner.

Horace wondered if it was a coincidence that her name just happened to be Angel. Her name meant messenger. Perhaps this was his brother's way of getting a message to him that he didn't have to live a life of solitude anymore. Here was his chance at redemption.

He was ready when Joey and Marlow exited the house and raced over to him. Once they were inside, he sped off after Joey read the address of where Angel was. He saw terror on Marlow's face. He wanted to reassure her that there was time to help Angel. He knew the story of Angel's first son and the guilt Marlow felt over that. He'd lived with his own share of guilt so he could relate. Not after today. It was time they all pulled themselves up by their boot straps and did what needed to be done. He was a part of this group now. It was time he stopped being on the outside just looking in. He needed to step up. He could help Marlow and Angel.

"Don't worry. Manny told me that his sister was the best. I just got a text that she needs the address to meet you there," he explained.

Horace handed his phone to Joey to text the address.

"Thank you, Horace. I can't thank you enough for this," Marlow spoke, nervously from the passenger seat.

"It's my pleasure. Let's focus on your sister and her baby. Nothing else matters."

"You know, my sister has been gambling with life for a long time. She's still so young, yet has been through so much. Topping that off, she has another baby? When did that happen? Why wouldn't she tell me that in all of the brief calls she's made over the past year to me? I have so many questions."

"Boo, don't beat yourself up over this. We're going to get all the answers you need. First, let's focus on Angel and trying to find out where her baby is. No way are we leaving either one of them in the system. You've had enough sleepless nights," Joey said.

"Any and everything I can do to help, lean on me. Angel isn't the only person who has gambled with their life. I could tell you both some things that would knock your socks off when I comes to my life and what I've been through. Maybe one day I will. For now, your sister is the priority. Let's bring your family back together."

Horace was focused because he meant every word of what he'd just said. He didn't know Angel. He'd never met her before. Something was speaking to him and telling him that his focus wasn't just the casino anymore. He had a real life to get to. It was starting today.

Get Horace and Angel's love story in, Love's Gamble,
now available for preorder at
https://www.amazon.com/dp/B0DL4MRNYG

About Love's Gamble:

Tightly wound casino owner, Horace Grant didn't know what family meant until the day his best friend Torrence called him brother. Finding his footing in life in Las Vegas, he put the word 'sin' in "Sin City" with the wicked relationships with women that came with having money and power. Soon, that was no longer enough for him. Making a move to Chicago, his newfound friends showed him what was missing from his life; real, true love.

Angel Reagan has been a lost soul for most of her adult life. For years, she'd been running away from facing the bleak reality of life without her son who died and a family who made her feel nothing but shame. Having unconditional love was never something in her grasp until she met Horace, a man who cared for her like no other.

Horace and Angel are two broken souls who discover that life may not come at them straight with no chasers, but love can break through even the smallest crack in concrete.

Can Horace, who knows everything about gambling, trust his next gamble on his heart?

Island Embers series.
Hunger for You
Desire for You
Thirst for You

What happens on the islands is supposed to stay on the islands but not when it comes to the Blackstone brothers who don't care who knows about their openly and unwavering love for their perfect women.

Preorder book two of the, *Island Embers* series, *Desire for You* for $4.99 before the price rises to $5.99 when released https://www.amazon.com/dp/B0DL4MKVRT

About Desire for You:
Byrum Blackstone is considered the one Blackstone brother who could not be tamed by any woman, no matter how salaciously desirable she is. That is, until he finds himself vulnerable to the one woman he should stay far away from; his executive assistant, Keiko Lee.

In the midst of fighting for her freedom and for custody of her son, Keiko vows to never trust another man with her heart. What she didn't expect was for her boss to offer her wicked, blood pressure spiking, hotter than she's ever known before nights of passion that stir her body and her heart back to life.

Neither Byrum nor Keiko are willing to admit their true feelings as the bigger problem of losing their careers overshadows how bittersweet newfound love could be not just in the present, but in the foreseeable future.

Be sure to get all seven books in the Brothers of Chi-Town series:

I Can't Let Go, Book 1

Carter Garrison vowed to love, honor and cherish his wife, Sienna, forsaking all others, something he forgot to do during a weekend of fun, bad company and poor judgement. Sienna Garrison never dreamed her college sweetheart, Carter, whom she pledged her life to, would break her heart and when he did, she moved out and moved on - or tried to. What better occasion is there than a friend's wedding to stir up old feelings and memories of love, intense passion and nights of sensual titillation. Gazes from across a room after almost two years apart revealed depths of love that had never died. Seeing Sienna again reminded Carter of what he'd lost and he vowed to never let go by doing whatever he could to get his wife back even if it included begging and pleading. Is Sienna ready to forgive and take a chance on life again with the only man she'd ever really loved? When Carter brings on the charm and turns up the heat, no woman is immune, especially Sienna.

Swagger and Baggage, Book 2

It's not a coincidence that casino owner, Torrence Allen, ran into his college sweetheart, Reese Michaels again; it's fate. As his memories unfold, he had tried everything to keep her in his life and his bed back then and failed at both. She wasn't ready for him then, but he hopes she is ready for him now.

Reese Michaels never thought she'd see Torrence again. Their split in college was dramatic and hurtful and still, no man had been able to win her heart. She considered herself the permanent third wheel to friends who had found love and marriage. Their whirlwind affair, quickly turned into love just as it suddenly crashed and burned when a woman shows up to claim Torrence as hers. When it's also revealed that this woman isn't the only 'other woman', Reese finds herself left with a broken heart, shattered love, and dreams of forever beyond her reach. How did she not know about the other part of Torrence's active and amorous life?

Torrence isn't ready to give up on having Reese in his life after his deceit. He finds himself in the fight of his life to finally have the love and commitment he wanted only with her. His swagger had always won women over, but it's his baggage that's causing his life to spiral out of control and he could once again find himself without the woman he has always loved.

Claiming His Child, Book 3

Business magnate Dexter Patterson refused to let anything keep him from checking off all of the boxes equating to achievement in life to prove that though he came from a rough childhood on the south side of Chicago, he still thrived and became a success. Looking around at those closest to him, Dexter found that he was still missing something...Love.

When aspiring model, Alyssa Kincaid met Dexter, she couldn't get enough of his sexual magnetism, fiery nights of passion, and secret rendezvous. She thought they were headed toward forever when a surprising call from him ended what they had causing her to leave Chicago, taking with her a secret.

Dexter thought that no woman could ever tame him, not even Alyssa who entranced him with her sexy body, smoky, sultry voice and untamed desire. Too little, too late, he realized he'd made a mistake by walking away and then she was gone. Time and distance didn't diminish the chemistry between them and the child Alyssa carried and never told him about had him in the fight of his life to win back her heart and the chance to have the family he'd always wanted.

Will Alyssa continue to curse kismet when Dexter suddenly reappears in her life or will she believe that his yearning for her isn't just because of their child, but because when she left Chicago, she took his heart with her?

Always Bet on Black, Book 4

Sexy, debonair, Delvin "DJ" "Black" Michaels, left Chicago as a man in search of a better life than the one he had where everyone knew him as "Black". He met a woman, fell in love, and then she turned out to be someone he didn't really know when her scandalous life ruined his career.

Avalon Hart had lived her life on the edge, making do the best way she knew how even if it meant scheming men out of their hard-earned money. She learned how to survive from the streets and she was a woman who had a way with men that got her whatever she wanted, that was until she encountered DJ Michaels in Chicago, a man from her past whom she had once easily swayed to her desires. She realized early that the man she encountered in New York had grown immune to her tricks, even the ones she learned how to do in bed that he loved so much.

DJ and Avalon are on a roller coaster ride to love and neither knew it. He had a lot to lose if he let Avalon get too close to him again. This time, whatever she was plotting, he was ready to take her down, even if it meant losing his heart in the process. He was betting on "Black" for the win, but so was Avalon, in her own way. There was no telling who would end up on top, but one thing was for sure – the road to getting there was going to be filled with hot, sexy fun, a pair of handcuffs and a whole lot of sensuality that neither could resist!

It Takes Two to Tangle, Book 5

Councilman Tucker Glass, a native of Chicago, has set his eyes on the biggest prize, that of Mayor of the city he has loved all of his life. At thirty-nine, his career spans back many years as a City Council member and then most recently, as City Council President. His resume reads like a ratings-topper novel full of accomplishments that make him more than qualified for the job, but what he wants to avoid is the drama that could block his path to the mayor's mansion. He's always been a strait-laced politician, but his personal life could spawn a real-life reality show complete with hair pulling, tongue-lashing and accusatory finger pointing which would all occur in the first episode. Tucker wasn't expecting his past to come back to haunt him just as he'd found the woman who was making his life complete. He would do anything to keep her in his life, but is he willing to give up his run for the mayor's office to keep that love in-tact? Nichelle Michaels didn't know that love could be so right until she met and fell in love with Tucker Glass, a man fourteen years older and wiser than her, but who showed her how a man should treat a woman, and that's after she spent the past year testing the water between how a man loves and how a woman loves. Now that she knows what she wants, a woman from Tucker's past could ruin her perfect love. Tucker and Nichelle are in love, but is he willing to risk his chance at being Mayor because his ex-wife, or the woman he thought was his ex-wife, wants to now be First Lady of Chicago? Was he really ready to tangle with a woman who specialized in drama every day on television as the star on the nation's number one reality show? Tucker may be ready for Chicago, but is Chicago ready for the drama that comes along with the popular politician?

Crashing Into Love, Book 6

His name is Joseph Kincaid and while most call him Joey, the women of Chicago call him a variety of sexy epithets that are too salacious to utter in public. He's a professional wrestler who is unmatched in the ring, untamed in his response to confrontation and unleashed when it comes to his bedroom proclivities, bringing women pleasure beyond their amorous fantasies. For the second time in her life, Marlow Warren was responsible for an accident that altered someone's life. The first time, she ran to avoid bringing disgrace to her family while hiding from her past, but this time, she's all about making amends to the man whose life she ruined. Everything changed when Joey and Marlow's lives collided and it wasn't all bad. Hurt, anger and unending apologies turned into lust, desire and unbridled cravings, something neither of them could fight. When Marlow's past arrives in a threatening way, Joey knew he would risk his life to protect her because he was now fighting for more than a future back in the ring; he was ready to fight for love.

Get the entire five-book series, The Sullivans of Montana, now available for your reading pleasure at https://www.amazon.com/dp/B09M41D76N?binding=kindle_edition&ref=dbs_dp_rwt_sb_pc_tkin

Also by Cheryl Barton
www.cherylbarton.net
Upcoming Novels
<u>**Romance**</u>

<u>**The Sullivans of Montana**</u>
Home for Thanksgiving
The Way You Love Me
On the Right Track
Three's a Crowd
The Law of Love

<u>**Sister Act**</u>
An Unexpected Destiny
For You I Will
More Than Friends

<u>**Bachelor Series**</u>
Bachelor Not for Sale
A Designed Affair
A Perfect Combination
Love at Last

<u>**A Lovers' Heart Series**</u>
Heartthrob
Heartbeat
Heartbreaker

<u>**Brothers of Chi-Town Series**</u>
I Can't Let Go
Swagger and Baggage
Claiming His Child
Always Bet on Black
It Takes Two to Tangle
Crashing into Love
Leaks, Lies, Lust and Love
Love's Gamble

<u>**Island Embers**</u>
Hunger for You
Desire for You
Thirst for you

Amorous Occupations
The Artist
The Bookkeeper
The Chef
The Dancer
The Electrician

Stand Alone Romance
Snowbound
Cupid's Arrow
One Wish
His Halloween Promise
Holly for Christmas
A Better Man
Bossy
Un-Break My Heart
Love on Top
Take a Knee
Love at First Sight
My First Love
Black Love
A Younger Man
One Moment in Time
The Lake House
True Lies or True Love
When I Think of You
And Then There Was You
Baby, Come Back
Unforgettable
The Power of Seduction
Seize the Moment
A Christmas Wish
It Should Have Been You
The Christmas Layover
The Sweetest Revenge
The Sweetest Temptation
The Diner
Dashing Through the Snow
A Trick and a Treat
Love Therapy
Mister Christmas

Upcoming Romance Releases

Sons of a Sullivan

*Wrath of a Sullivan

Upcoming Urban Drama

*Amerikka

Inspirational Romance Series

When God Says Yes
Rescue Me
Release Me
*Restore Me

Inspirational Series

Encouraging Words From One Sister to Another
One Sister Away, Volume 1
One Sister Away, Volume 2
One Sister Away, Volume 3
One Sister Away, Volume 4

Inspirational Standalone
A Letter to My Mother
Straightening Her Crown

About the Author

Cheryl Barton lives in Maryland and in her spare time she loves to read espionage, crime and romance novels, cook, watch Sci-fi movies, spend time with family and friends and enjoy Maryland steamed crabs.
Cheryl is the author of over forty romance novels, four inspirational novels and is proud of six book compilation projects with several other incredible women.
Cheryl was a 2019 Finalist for the Emma Award given by Romance Slam Jam and a 2018 Finalist for the Literary Trailblazer of the Year award by the Indie Author Legacy Award.

Cheryl's books are available on her website as well as www.bn.com, www.amazon.com and www.kobo.com

Connect with Cheryl Barton
Author Cheryl Barton website
www.cherylbarton.net
Amazon Author Page
www.amazon.com/author/cherylbarton
Instagram: @cherylbartonbooks
Twitter: @cbartonbooks
Facebook: @cherylbartonbooks
TikTok: @bookbabecb
Threads: @cherylbartonbooks@threads.net